Princesses of Palosia

Sisters torn between love and duty...

Princess Sofia and Princess Rosa have their futures
mapped out for them. They've been brought up to marry
well for the benefit of their country; finding a partner of
their own and falling in love is not even a consideration!
But when the time comes to do their royal duty, love
unexpectedly finds *them*, throwing the future of their
marriages—and the crown—into crisis!

Will finding true love give these princesses
the courage to defy their father and fight for their own
fairy-tale ending?

Find out in

Secret Royal's Napoli Reunion
by Nina Milne

Billionaire Marco doesn't even realize he's lost his heart
to a princess when he falls for his long-lost love, Sofia,
all over again!

And

Conveniently Engaged to a Princess
by Suzanne Merchant

The pressure is on for Rosa to marry for duty,
but what happens when she unexpectedly falls in love
with her convenient fiancé, Count Luca?

Both available now!

Dear Reader,

As I wrote this story, the word *regret* came into my head a lot; I really didn't want Marco or Sofia to feel regret. They have both had to cope with tough things in their lives, things that have made them distrust the power of love. This story is about Marco and Sofia helping each other navigate a path to letting go of regret, finding positives and ultimately trusting in the power of love. I hope you enjoy reading how they made their way along that path.

Nina x

SECRET ROYAL'S NAPOLI REUNION

NINA MILNE

Harlequin

ROMANCE

Harlequin®
ROMANCE

ISBN-13: 978-1-335-47055-3

Secret Royal's Napoli Reunion

Copyright © 2025 by Nina Milne

Recycling programs
for this product may
not exist in your area.

Harlequin Enterprises ULC
22 Adelaide St. West, 41st Floor
Toronto, Ontario M5H 4E3, Canada
www.Harlequin.com

HarperCollins Publishers
Macken House, 39/40 Mayor Street Upper,
Dublin 1, D01 C9W8, Ireland
www.HarperCollins.com

Printed in U.S.A.

Nina Milne has always dreamed of writing for Harlequin Romance—ever since she played libraries with her mother's stacks of Harlequin romances as a child. On her way to this dream, Nina acquired an English degree, a hero of her own, three gorgeous children and—somehow!—an accountancy qualification. She lives in Brighton and has filled her house with stacks of books—her very own *real* library.

Books by Nina Milne

Harlequin Romance

Royal Sarala Weddings

His Princess on Paper
Bound by Their Royal Baby

Summer Escapes

Their Mauritius Wedding Ruse

The Christmas Pact

Snowbound Reunion in Japan

Winter Escapes

Cinderella's Moroccan Midnight Kiss

Falling for His Stand-In Fiancée
Consequence of Their Dubai Night
Wedding Planner's Deal with the CEO

Visit the Author Profile page
at Harlequin.com for more titles.

To Suman: You are an inspiration.
You always find the positives.

Praise for
Nina Milne

PROLOGUE

Seven years ago

MARCO OPENED HIS EYES, aware of an unfamiliar sense of anticipation, a knowledge that the day ahead held something precious. He stared up at the ceiling, memories of the previous days ranging through his head, felt his smile widen as he thought of Sonia.

Not that he believed his unexpected visitor, the young woman he'd rescued from unwanted attentions on the streets of Naples, was truly called Sonia. As for a surname, she had refused to give one, said she had no wish to know his either. So, days after he had brought her back to his student digs he was none the wiser; all he suspected was that Sonia was running away from something or someone.

All he knew was that somehow the dark-haired nineteen-year-old, with her rare smile and expressive blue eyes, had got under his skin and he liked her, truly liked her. Wanted to protect her, make her smile, be with her. Hoped that as time went on Sonia could be persuaded to trust him with the truth of who she was. Maybe even today, after the kiss they had shared the previous night, a kiss that had been so glorious, so beautiful that his whole body, his heart, his soul was still buzzing with the after-effects.

What could they do today? Plans fizzed through his head; even as he reminded himself that he should be going to university, that lectures awaited. But for once he couldn't bring himself to care—he'd catch up. He enjoyed his course, had chosen international business management because he knew he would need a sensible job whilst he pursued his real dream. A dream to become a sculptor, to follow in the footsteps of Italy's famous artists. To this end he had undertaken courses in pottery, blacksmithing, jewellery making, sculpting. As many as he could afford, financed by a part-time job in a local artist's shop. But today not even his current project could lure him. Right now, nothing was more important than Sonia.

A sudden question entered his head. Was this how his father had once felt about his mother, this elation, this joy? He blinked the thought away; he wasn't going to get carried away by this, whatever this was. But neither was he going to compare it to whatever his parents had once had. Because his parents' love had withered and shrivelled, leaving behind nothing but the fruit of bitter regret.

But that was irrelevant, those were thoughts he didn't want to harbour. Not today, when the day stretched before him, before them. Perhaps he could take Sonia to see the botanical gardens; she had mentioned that her sister loved gardens, the one bit of information she had dropped.

Outside the early morning sunshine scattered the sky with motes of yellow and orange and he decided to get up. He'd go to the bakery and bring back the *sfogliatelle* pastries that she loved for breakfast.

An hour later Marco surveyed his efforts with approval. The shell-shaped pastries with their creamy filling were carefully arranged on the table, alongside a bunch of flowers. The smell of freshly brewing coffee beans pervaded the air. But there was no sign of Sonia. Qualms touched him; had their kiss spooked her? The anxiety tautened—after the time they had spent together, the hours wrapped in each other's company, surely she knew he would never do anything she didn't want? That he wanted to help her, for her to trust him. He hadn't meant to kiss her, but he hadn't been able to help himself. They'd been standing overlooking the panoramic vista of Naples, the stretch of history from the ancient fourteenth-century bell tower to the towering recent skyscrapers all bathed in the orange glow of a glorious sunset. She'd looked up at him to ask a question, her long dark hair ruffled in the breeze, her blue eyes sparkling, and temptation had been too much. He'd leant down and a tentative brush of his lips against hers had evolved, deepened into the type of kiss that fairy tales were made of.

That had been yesterday and they'd walked back, hand in hand, in a dazed silence neither had wanted to break. And he'd been so sure that the magic of the kiss would cast its spell onto this day, onto the future. But now that certainty faded with each tick of the clock; he glanced at his watch and then headed to the spare room, knocked gently on the door. No answer. He knocked again, louder. Still nothing. Worry and foreboding twisted inside him as he tried the door. Not locked; he had no idea if Sonia locked the door at night or not. A moment's hesitation and he pushed the door open and stepped over the threshold. The room was empty.

Marco strode over to the wardrobe, pulled

the door open. Nothing. He spun round; the bed was made. Walking over to the desk, he searched for a note, a clue, any indication of what had happened. The window was open and he stared outside; had she snuck out through there? Anxiety clenched his gut. Where would she have gone? Turning, he raced to the bed, stripped it down, searched for something, anything. Perhaps the note had slipped to the floor. Surely, she wouldn't have just left. Oh God. Was it his fault? He shouldn't have kissed her.

But no matter how frantic his search, all Marco found was a single strand of jet-black hair.

CHAPTER ONE

Present day

PRINCESS SOFIA OF PALOSIA stared at her reflection in the mirror, decked out in all her bridal finery. The duchess satin dress was straight from a fairy tale, designed to combine elegance with luxury, with a hand-beaded, long-sleeved bodice, corseted waist and a full ivory skirt that fell in soft folds to just brush the floor. To complete the picture-perfect image, an extravagant train extended behind her, to be held by the array of bridesmaids assembled to showcase the aristocracy from both the bride's and groom's sides.

Was she really going to do this? Sofia gritted her teeth, clenched her hands into fists. Yes, she was. She'd thought this through and marriage to Prince Eduardo of Sarcos was the only choice.

The alternative was to remain on Palosia,

trapped by her father into an existence, a life-style she didn't want. She loved her country, surrounded by the sparkling blue of the Mediterranean, the island a quixotic blend of so many terrains. Majestic-peaked mountains touched the skyline, sun-kissed beaches swathed with white sand stretched along the lapping waves. There were lush olive groves and valleys where fish-laden rivers flowed. The lazy drone of bees hummed in the flower-scented air. Palosia was a truly beautiful place. But there was no future for Sofia here.

Here she was hedged in by rules and restrictions, not allowed to pursue a career. Largely ignored but wheeled out on public occasions because, to her father's irritation, the people loved her. Despite the fact she had commoners' blood running through her veins. Despite the fact her mother had brought scandal and disrepute to the royal name. Perhaps the people felt pity for the princess who had been abandoned by her mother. The then Queen Flavia had run away, fled her distasteful marriage and gone back to the arms of her true love when Sofia was a baby.

And King Fiero had never forgiven his daughter for the humiliation of her mother's desertion. So, he in turn did his best to humiliate Sofia, had even written her out of the line of succession. Women could not rule in Palosia, but King Fiero had excluded Sofia completely, decreed that any sons born to her could not ascend the throne either.

Sofia could still taste the revelation of that bitter truth, when she'd learnt what he'd done. Had wondered if her mother could have envisaged the depth of King Fiero's anger when she'd fled, back—so it was rumored—to Naples.

Naples.

The word evoked the memories she had buried deep down, summoned images of Marco. The boy, the man, who had rescued her, taken her in and with whom she had shared her first kiss. His lips against hers, diffident at first and then...demanding, glorious. It was a kiss that had awoken desire, had dizzied her head, touched her heart, heated her body with unfamiliar sensations.

Not now. Now she was about to marry a prince. Create an alliance. Escape Palosia and hopefully she and Eduardo would be happy together. Have a family. There was no question of love. They both understood that, both happy with the idea of building a union based on convenience, liking and respect. A marriage that would work, unlike her parents'. That marriage had been based on one-sided love. King

Fiero had been smitten by Flavia's beauty. Had wooed and pursued, showered her with gifts and promises of wealth and power for her and her family and she had eventually agreed.

But she had never forgotten her true love and in the end that love had won. Had trumped her maternal love for Sofia, assuming she in fact felt any. Perhaps she hadn't. Perhaps she couldn't love a daughter begotten by a man she had grown to loathe.

Sofia didn't know, but she did know that love turned your head, messed up your priorities, made you act in ways that were wrong. And she wanted none of it.

There was a gentle knock at the door and she turned as her half-sister, Rosabella, known as Rosa, entered. A familiar wave of protective love surged over Sofia, along with worry at leaving Rosa. An anxiety she doused— reminding herself that her little sister was twenty-three now, would be twenty-four in the not too distant future. Plus the possibility that Rosa's mother, Queen Chiara, would repeat history and flee an unhappy marriage was now over. Gone too was any real danger that their father would divorce or banish Chiara; he knew the people wouldn't stand for it. So, it was finally okay to leave the sister who meant so very much to her. Rosa was the reason that Sofia had buckled down and submitted for so long to her father's tyrannies.

But now she would still see Rosa on visits to Palosia and perhaps the king would allow Rosa to visit Sofia on Sarcos. Still, the anxiety persisted, deepened, when she saw her sister's worried face.

For a moment illogical hope sprung—maybe something had happened, a reason to postpone the wedding? She shook the feeling away, reminded herself that this marriage was her salvation. A chance to build a life, to *have* a life. A chance to pursue her interest in interior design, even if she was only allowed to decorate and furnish a single royal residence. On Sarcos she could hopefully make a difference, work for good. Achieve something. Not be sidelined any more. Most importantly she hoped to be a parent, a good mother, whose head could never be turned by love, who would stand by her children through thick and thin.

Rosa stepped forward. 'There's someone here to see you. A woman. She managed to get through to the gardens. I was getting some fresh flowers for your bouquet and there she was. She asked to see you. I know I should have called security, but there is something about her. I think you should see her.'

Sofia nodded, trusted Rosa's opinion. 'It will

have to be quick, but bring her now and you stay in the antechamber, make sure no one interrupts us.'

Minutes later Rosa returned, accompanied by a heavily veiled young woman.

When they were alone the woman stepped forward. 'Thank you for seeing me.' Her voice soft, her accent a regional one. 'I…need, you need to know something.' She lifted her veil to reveal a sweetly pretty heart-shaped face, with cornflower-blue eyes smudged with tiredness.

'Go ahead.' Foreboding trickled through her, but Sofia kept her voice even, wanted her visitor to feel able to speak freely.

'Prince Eduardo loves me. I love him. This marriage to you, he believes it is his duty to go through with it, but…what about his duty to me?' The woman turned wide anguished eyes to Sofia. 'He doesn't know, but I am pregnant.'

The words echoed as Sofia forced her brain to assimilate their meaning, to think logically.

'How do I know this is true?'

'I have pictures, messages. I swear to you, Your Highness, that what I say is true. I understand the importance of a political alliance but what about the baby? What will become of him or her? Perhaps it is right to sacrifice my happiness and Eduardo's but I will not sacrifice my child's. So, I have come to you. I cannot get to Eduardo and he will not take my calls.'

This could not be happening and for a craven instant Sofia wanted to cover her ears, close her eyes, in the hope this was some sort of hallucination. But she knew it wasn't. Intuition told her that this woman was speaking the truth, but logic told her she might not be. She had to keep her dignity, keep her cool, push down both panic and the impetuosity that was telling her to simply get up and run. Or better yet, put this woman into the wedding dress and send her in her place.

The bottom line was if this woman was telling truth Sofia could not go through with this marriage. Would not enter a rerun of her own parents' marriage. Her mother should never have agreed to marry King Fiero when she loved another and King Fiero should never have married a woman he knew to be in love with someone else. Sofia would not make the same mistake. Especially not when there was a baby involved. She'd been abandoned by her mother, understood the bitterness and the pain that ensued; she wouldn't allow this baby to suffer a similar fate.

'What is your name?' she asked

'Luciana.' The woman met her gaze. 'What are you going to do?' She placed her hand on her stomach as if to protect her child from whatever was to come next.

'I am going to call Eduardo.' She kept her gaze on Luciana's face, saw her flinch slightly and then straighten.

'Will you tell him about the baby?'

'No. But I think you should.'

Sofia pressed the button, held the phone to her ear. 'Eduardo. I have Luciana with me. She wishes to tell you something.'

There was a silence on the other end, a silence that spoke volumes.

'I'll pass you over.'

'Sofia…wait, I need to explain…'

'You need to talk to Luciana.'

She handed the phone over, aware that her nails were digging into her palms as she watched. Wondered why she wasn't more distraught, assumed it was because there was no love involved. The betrayal was still real and she knew the hurt would come later, along with an assessment of the consequences, but now that wasn't important as she watched Luciana's face, heard the tremble in her voice.

'Eduardo. It is me. I… I need you to know. I am pregnant.'

She couldn't hear his reply; it no longer mattered. She knew what she needed to know. and that meant she knew what she needed to do next.

One hour later...

'You've done what?' Rosa's brown eyes were wide open in shock.

'I've called off the wedding,' Sofia repeated.

'But Father will be furious, he is going to…' Rosa trailed off, clearly unable to even picture the extent of King Fiero's potential rage.

'I know.' Sofia tried to find some courage, told herself that she had no choice, even though she knew that no one else would see it that way. Especially not her father. Even Rosa looked shocked. But, 'I can't go through with it. Please help me out of this dress.' The feel of the material was restrictive, confining, a weight she wanted to be rid of. 'If I have to face the music, I would rather face it in clothes I can run in.' She tried to smile, knew the joke had fallen flat, because there was every chance she would have to run.

But before Rosa could even move towards her, the bedroom door crashed open and King Fiero strode in, his face apoplectic with rage. Various court officials hurried in after him, along with palace security and Queen Chiara, her face even paler than usual. The queen glanced first towards her daughter then at Sofia with worry writ large on her face.

'Is this true?' the king demanded. 'Eduardo has told me the wedding has been cancelled.'

'Yes, it's true. I have called the marriage off. Prince Eduardo is aware of my reasons, but the official line is that I have been taken ill.' Sofia had no intention of betraying Luciana's story, would leave it to Eduardo to make the decision as to how much of the truth to reveal.

'Pshaw…not a soul is going to believe that. Every court official knows you were ready to head to the church.'

'An illness is better than the truth.'

'There is no illness. And I have no wish to know the truth. Because it is irrelevant. Eduardo will still marry you if his father and I tell him to, despite this fiasco. He knows what is due to his country.'

'But… *I* cannot marry *him*.'

'Why not?' The timid intervention came from the queen.

The king swung round and Chiara flinched. Years of marital bullying and rage had prepared her for what was now a ritual humiliation. 'Be silent, woman. I do not care why not.' He turned back to Sofia. 'I am telling you right here and now, you will go to that chapel and marry the prince.'

For a moment she almost agreed, just as she had agreed to whatever had been demanded of her all her life. Oh, she tried to stand up to her father, tried at the very least to stand between him and Rosa, but, in the end, King Fiero held power over all of them. Apart from that one rebellious week of escape in Naples, when she had temporarily broken free of her father's control. The memory gave her a sudden surge of courage. Eduardo might be willing to sacrifice love for duty but Sofia had seen what happened when a one-sided marriage went wrong. Did she want Luciana's unborn child to pay the price she herself had paid? The answer was no. So somehow, she had to stand up to her father.

'No, I will not. This marriage is wrong. It would bring unhappiness to too many.'

'Unhappiness?' the king raged. 'You are indeed your mother's daughter, mewling and whining about happiness. A commoner through and through, your blood even more tainted than I believed. I always knew you weren't a true princess and yet I gave you one chance to do something for your country. And you have failed me. If you refuse to behave as a princess, your title will be rescinded and you will be banished, like your mother before you. You will leave Palosia tonight and you will not return.'

'Leave?' Sofia faltered; the idea filled her head with fear. How could she leave Rosa with no prospect of seeing her again? On a practical note, how would she survive? She had no money, no real knowledge of how the world away from Palosia worked. The royal family had wealth but that was controlled by her father. He paid her bills, granted her a small monthly allowance and had consistently vetoed any idea she had come up with to earn her own money. The only qualification she had she had obtained from an online interior design course that she had done in secret.

Panic pounded her temples, yet buried in the strum of anxiety was a barely discernible note of exhilaration at the prospect of freedom.

Her father nodded. 'Yes. Leave.' He turned to his security chief. 'Remove Princess Sofia from this palace. I want her to be off the island within twelve hours.'

There was a murmur of consternation from the courtiers and Rosa stepped forward. Instantly Sofia shook her head at her sister; she did not want the king's wrath to fall on Rosa.

'But, sire, the press…' The words from a chief counsellor.

'The people…' This from another advisor.

'They will see that Sofia has disgraced and humiliated our country.'

Sofia dug her nails into her palm as she heard the murmurs of agreement, realised that to all these spectators it looked as though she had thrown away political gain, a marriage that would have helped her country. Her father and Eduardo's had made a lucrative trade deal that was to be cemented by the marriage. A deal that would now be in jeopardy.

'I do not want to see her face. Carry out my orders.' The king turned. 'Chiara, Rosabella, come with me.'

'Could I stay to help Sofia pack?' Rosa's voice was small. 'It may be better to keep things in the family.'

The king hesitated. 'You have half an hour.'

They waited until the room emptied, the security guard positioned outside, and Rosa headed to her, deftly starting to help her remove the bridal gown.

'Sofia, what are you going to do?' Sofia could see the worry, anxiety and doubts in her sister's eyes, wanted to allay all three.

'I am going to go and have an adventure,' Sofia said. 'I will not let Father ruin my life. I am sure at some point he will allow me back. The people will not like my banishment to be for ever.'

'But how?' Rosa stepped back. 'I will give you all the money I have but it is not enough. Where will you go?'

Incipient panic threatened again. She had

to go somewhere. A choice had to be made. Her brain scrambled together a plan: she would complete the mission she had been forced to cease seven years before. She would find her mother. Return to Naples.

But it wasn't Flavia who came to mind—after all the only image she had of her mother was constructed from her own imagination and Internet research. When she thought of Naples she thought of a young man with over-long blond hair, grey eyes, a passion for sculpture, and she thought of a magical sunset kiss.

But that wasn't why she would return. She didn't even know Marco's surname. He had been a student in Naples, and could be anywhere in the world right now. But Naples was where she would go.

'I will be all right,' she told Rosa. 'I will get a job. I'll manage. On my own two feet.' She glanced at her watch. 'Now I must pack and you must go. Before Father turns his anger on you. It is better if you don't know where I am going.'

She stepped forward and hugged her sister, just as the guard knocked on the door.

Four days later...

Marco Stewart glanced at his watch and quickened his stride as he headed for the upmarket estate agency situated in the centre of Naples. He was en route to pick up the keys for the villa he'd purchased, not so much for himself but for his mother and her husband. The man he supposed was technically his stepfather, even though his mother had married Lorenzo only five years before when Marco was twenty-three.

His mother would protest at the purchase but Marco knew she would love it and he wanted her to be happy; after all, Giulia had sacrificed a lot for him. Both his parents had. And despite the knowledge it wasn't his fault, he couldn't eradicate the guilt he felt.

His parents were individually both wonderful, loving parents. But as a couple they'd brought out the worst in each other. Marco had never understood it. Once his parents had undoubtedly been in love—their wedding photos showed two people who thought the world of each other. Yet somehow that love had died, leaving behind a scorched earth, a place where even civility became an impossibility. Marco's childhood had been experienced against a backdrop of constant drama, screaming matches, tears, thrown ornaments and insults. Where he was always in the middle, an unwilling referee, in a constant attempt not to be caught in the crossfire or, worse, still have to pick a side.

He'd asked them once what had happened, to be met with a shrug. 'Who knows? Love couldn't survive real life, I suppose. Bills, nappy changing, responsibilities.' And, 'I mistook attraction for compatibility. I think your father missed Scotland.' The place Alec Stewart had been born and grown up in, until a work placement to Rome where he'd met Giulia and fallen in love. But long after love died, Marco's dad had remained in Italy for Marco's sake, spent decades away from the homeland he missed. Another layer to Marco's guilt.

But despite everything they were amazing parents; Marco had never felt unloved or unwanted or a burden. What he did feel was guilt at the knowledge that his parents had stayed together for him, embroiled in an ever downward spiral of misery, but determined to remain together for Marco's sake. So that all Marco had wanted to do was grow up, to enable his parents to be freed of the misery of their marriage.

Which they had duly done as soon as he'd finished university. His dad had returned to Scotland, bought a remote place in the Highlands.

And his mother was happily remarried, to a widower who had a brood of children, all grown up but they had welcomed his mother in with open arms and she seemed to have become one of them, absorbed into a close-knit happy family. Something she had always wanted; another reason for Marco's guilt. He'd known his mother would have loved to have more children, but she had given that up for him.

But at least now she was happy; he recalled her excited voice as she discussed her step-daughter. 'Louisa and Juan are expecting a baby. It will feel like being a gran…' Then her voice had trailed off. 'I am sorry, Marco. I…'

'It's okay, Mum. I am happy for you and for them. Say congratulations from me.'

And he *was* happy for them, though the news had prodded the hurt, the pain that he had tried to bury over the past three years. Had brought back memories of Leo, the baby he'd believed to be his son. He closed his eyes, grounded himself. That was over. Leo was not his son, and never had been. All that was left were the memories of those precious six months when he'd thought he was a father. Now all he could do for Leo was to stay away, allow him to live his life with his real father.

As for Marco, he had spent the last three years focused on becoming a success. Rich beyond belief. A life where he could mingle with the rich and famous, could buy whatever he wanted…including this villa.

As he neared the estate agency, he saw a woman standing outside looking in the window, a woman with a cascade of dark hair, a way of standing, straight-backed, graceful, but as though she were always poised to run.

The sight triggered a memory of a woman he'd once known, and never forgotten.

His feet dragged to a stop; his heart hammered his chest even as his brain told him to cool it. How many times had this happened to him before? A glimpse of a dark-haired woman, a certain sway of the hips, a certain way of lifting a hand to tuck a tendril of hair behind an ear…and in seven years the woman had never been the woman he'd hoped it would be. The woman he'd worried about, had sleepless nights over. For months after Sonia's disappearance, he'd scoured the streets of Naples, revisited every place they had ever been, but all to no avail. He'd painted all sorts of scenarios, terrified that their kiss had driven her away to some awful fate. In the end, he could only hope that she had found sanctuary elsewhere.

Now…he remained still, watched the woman, waited for the inevitable disappointment as she turned away from the window, saw her profile and almost froze before urgency

propelled him forward and he heard his voice.
'Excuse me. *Scusi.*'

The woman turned and now he did freeze,
as her dark blue eyes widened.

'Sonia?'

CHAPTER TWO

SOFIA'S TUMMY WENT into freefall, instincts colliding, fight versus flight, but her feet seemed rooted to the pavement, the two of them caught in an immoveable tableau of shock. Could it really be Marco? But as she stood here, looking at him, every bone in her body told her it was. Even though this man was a far cry from the young man of yesteryear. The over-long hair was now cut ruthlessly short, his features seemed harder, the jaw more pugnacious, the grey eyes full of shock.

Now her gaze lingered on his lips, set in a firm line. Lips that had given her such joy in that one glorious kiss. 'Marco?' The more her gaze drank him in, the more familiar he looked, and for once all the years of royalty, of knowing the right thing to say at the right time, the correct smile, the things drilled into her in lieu of an actual education, deserted her and she knew she resembled nothing more than a puffer fish. 'I…'

He took a deep breath and relief dawned in his eyes at the unspoken confirmation that it was really her. 'You're okay?' he asked. 'Thank God. All these years I've wondered, hoped… that you were all right.'

'I'm fine.' As she looked at him, still hardly able to believe that this was Marco, she became aware of something she couldn't quite define: a beat of her pulse, a race of her heart and an almost irresistible urge to step closer to him. 'I didn't think you'd even remember me.' The inanity of the words struck her as she saw his expression change, relief now mitigated by incredulity.

'Not remember you? You vanished without trace. I was worried sick.'

Sofia tried to work out what to say. 'Sorry. I don't know why I said that. Maybe I hoped you'd forget about me.' The only way to mitigate the guilt she'd felt at the impossibility of explaining the circumstances of her rapid departure. An explanation that was still not possible. All she could think of to do was to close this down as quickly as possible. 'I am truly sorry that you were worried, but now, as you can see, I am fine so, if you'll excuse me, I'd better be on my way.'

'Huh? You're kidding, right? You're going to go, disappear again?' Now a hint of anger entered the mix and he took a deep breath and, with what was a clear effort, he stepped back, hands raised in the air, ran a hand over his face, and when he spoke his voice was softer and she glimpsed *her* Marco, the man she had remembered for all these years, tucked away in a small private space in her heart. Her secret—she'd never told anyone about Marco, not even Rosa. 'Look, I'm incredibly relieved that you are okay, but after all these years I guess I would like some explanation for what happened. Especially…'

He broke off and she became aware of a woman waving at him through the estate agency window. 'I have an appointment. It shouldn't take long or I can postpone.'

Sofia turned away from the window slightly; so far there had been no publicity about her race from the altar, but there had been some publicity about the engagement and she had no wish to be recognised.

'So, give me five minutes and then how about a quick catch-up over a coffee? A latte, extra milky with chocolate sprinkles.'

'You remember?' The idea surprised and warmed her.

'I do.' And in that instant, something

changed, crackled in the air, fizzed and popped. Marco remembered how much she had loved the local lattes—what else did he remember? Right now, as their gazes met she'd put money he was walking the same steps down memory lane. To a kiss that was seared on her memory. But surely not on his. To him it must have long since faded to insignificance. He must have kissed hundreds of women since then.

Whereas she…well, never mind the actual statistic. Because the only other person she had ever kissed was Eli… The memory caused distaste, the bitter tang of betrayal, the knowledge of her own foolishness, and she pushed it away.

'And you have a double espresso with a drop of milk. And I said…'

'That you couldn't see the point.' His eyes rested on her face and he gave a sudden smile, and Sofia blinked. His smile had always made her want to smile as well, but now, seven years later, it did more than that. It made her tummy dip, her toes curl, and heated her whole body. 'So, what do you say? One coffee for old times' sake?'

She should turn and walk away. That made sense. Because she couldn't give him what he wanted—couldn't explain the truth without revealing her identity. And she had no intention of doing that. For some reason the press hadn't so much as mentioned the jilting of a prince at the altar; instead, there had been a brief statement from the Palosian palace that Princess Sofia had been taken suddenly ill, that the family would appreciate privacy at this difficult time. Accompanied by a picture of Prince Eduardo, his face etched with concern. Though knowing what she knew, Sofia wondered exactly who the concern was for. Not for her, she was sure.

She didn't know what was going on, assumed it was a publicity spin, in which case the best thing she could do was to stay under the radar. At least until she found her mother; she had no wish to bring the glare of publicity down on Flavia, and had no wish for the press to interrogate her as to her reasons for ending her engagement. Problem was, the real world was hard to navigate if you were unable to show a passport or proof of identity. If you didn't want to admit to who you were.

So coffee was a bad idea. Yet temptation beckoned. Put it down to loneliness, to wanting human contact, wanting a distraction, or perhaps sheer curiosity. She wanted to know what he had done with his life. He seemed harder but he'd also clearly done well for himself. Her practised eye discerned the discreetly expensive cut of his clothes, the equally discreet brand that displayed wealth but without the need to be ostentatious about it. Maybe this chance meeting was fate, an opportunity to put the past to rest.

'One coffee sounds good, but I can't offer any explanation. I'm sorry.' And she was; his concern was undoubtedly genuine and the idea that he had cared was…nice.

Understandable confusion creased his brow and then there was that smile again. 'I know now that you are safe and well and unharmed. That will have to be good enough. Seven years ago, if I'd been offered that I'd have taken it. One coffee, no explanations it is. Give me a minute. Or you can come in?'

Sofia shook her head. 'I'll wait.'

She watched as he went inside, the easy stride, the breadth of his shoulders, saw the woman smile at him, an exchange of words, and then Marco frowned, the woman looked apologetic and then he smiled again, she handed over an envelope and then he turned and headed back to the door, pushed it open and her gaze dwelled on the shape of his forearm, the strength of his hands.

And Sofia admitted the truth to herself. She also wanted to prolong this contact because something she'd only latently recognised in her youth was glaringly obvious now. This man was gorgeous. Now qualms surfaced; perhaps coffee was a bad idea. Marco might be gorgeous but that was irrelevant. She was in Naples to find her mother, and learn how to live her own life, stand on her own two feet. Not to be distracted by good looks and an amazing body. Seven years ago, attraction had distracted her, made her lose perspective. But she hadn't identified it as attraction back then. Back then all she had known was a consuming desire to be with Marco, with the young man who was so passionate and so kind, who'd looked at her as if she mattered, as if she was important. Now she could dimly perceive that the tug, the connection she felt, was physical.

And she still had no idea how to navigate the shoals of attraction and no desire to learn. Attraction was too complicated a landscape; her mother's beauty had been what caught King Fiero's eye, caused him to fall in love and pursue a woman who didn't want him.

'Ready?' Marco's deep voice cut through the thoughts.

Get a grip; she was going for one coffee. 'Ready. That was quick.'

'I just needed to pick up some keys; the agent had also said she could find me an interior designer, but it turns out he's not available after all.'

Sofia opened her mouth and closed it again. She could hardly offer her services, based on an online course and a sketchbook full of ideas. The idea was preposterous. She had no experience, no website, no references; hell, she couldn't even tell him her true name.

So, she remained silent as they negotiated a busy road with its preponderance of cars weaving and merging, cheerful horns blaring as scooters zoomed in and out in the organised chaos that characterised the city's traffic flow. Then made their way down a couple of narrow alleyways, strung with washing pegged out to dry, walls bedecked with posters and graffiti, and balconies dotted with vibrant potted flowers. The walk triggered an avalanche of memories, of seven years ago when they had walked together along similar streets. The contrast seemed stark; back then she'd felt as if she were floating on air in his company, they'd spoken about so many things or walked in a silence that had been so full of contentment there had been no need for words. But then, as now, she'd always been achingly aware of him, his proximity, only then she hadn't understood the significance of her feelings.

Not until he'd kissed her, his lips unlocking the answer, unleashing a burn of need, one they had never had a chance to explore. And never would.

It somehow seemed important to remember that as they reached a bustling café, joined the throng of customers, and she was even more aware of his proximity, the hard swell of muscle, the breadth of his shoulders. Tried to focus instead on the aroma of coffee and baking, the bricked arches behind the glass-fronted cabinets that housed an array of pastries, the foliage and flowers that wreathed the ceiling above.

'I'll get the coffees,' he said. 'Would you like something to eat?' His grey eyes way too discerning.

'Just coffee is fine,' she said, even as she tried to remember when she'd last eaten. Her appetite had vanished in the aftermath of her furtive departure from Palosia, the need to find a cheap place to stay, the dawning realisation that finding a job of any sort was difficult without a useable bank account, any form of identity. But she was managing. She was staying in a cheap hotel and working night shifts as a cleaner for cash. Thankfully on her own, so no one could see how much longer it took her than the allocated hours. Simply due to inexperience. But it was a job, her first job, and she felt a sense of pride in it, a thrill at receiving money she'd earnt. 'I'll grab a table.'

A few minutes later he made his way over.

'I brought food,' he said. 'I couldn't resist.'

She opened her mouth to protest and then she saw the tray he placed down on the table and as if on cue her tummy gave a rumble of hunger.

'*Sfogliatelle,*' she said.

More memories washed over her, of other cafés, of ending up with cream from the pastry on her upper lip, the feel of his finger gently rubbing it off. 'Thank you,' she managed. 'I'll give you some money.'

He shook his head. 'No. You didn't ask for them. Anyway, I skipped lunch. It's as much for me as you.'

'Then thank you,' she said, aware that she was suddenly ravenous. Had a suspicion it was because for the first time in days she felt safe, even though she knew that didn't really make sense. Or maybe it did, because that was how he had made her feel seven years ago. Safe. She reached for a pastry.

Marco watched as she ate, realised that Sonia, or whatever her name was, had been hungry, whatever she had said. He studied her face, saw how her beauty had matured, her face more slender, the slant of her cheekbones more accentuated, a few more lines around the arresting dark blue eyes. Her hair was longer, fell in sleek waves past her shoulders. His gaze went back to her face and now he couldn't help but focus on her lips, generous and, oh, so kissable. Did she remember their kiss? Or had she wiped it from her memory because that had triggered her to run away? *Forget the kiss.* Curiosity resurfaced. What had happened seven years before? Maybe a better question would be, why did it matter? She had said she was fine. All that had happened was that she'd moved on. And yet…he studied her face again, saw the smudges of tiredness under her eyes, and the questions kept coming. How could he have got it so wrong? Why couldn't she explain now? Tell him she'd regretted their kiss and so she'd done a midnight runner. And why did his instinct tell him something was wrong?

Stop it, Marco. Surely he knew by now that his knight-errant instincts were misplaced. When he'd met Leila, she'd purported to being down on her luck, the victim of a bad breakup. He'd taken her story at face value, agreed to let her stay in his spare room. That had been the start of a path that had led to a world of grief and pain.

He wouldn't do that again; Sonia had said she was fine, so he'd make polite conversation and be on his way. 'What brings you back to Naples? A holiday?'

'Business,' she said, but didn't elaborate. 'What about you? Tell me about yourself,' she said. 'Did you graduate? Are you a sculptor now?'

'No.' The question a bolt from the past; he'd long since abandoned those ambitions and dreams. Dreams he'd harboured since childhood, when he'd made things out of putty, out of clay, cardboard tubes, anything. Models, building blocks... It had been a way of blocking out his parents' arguments, the accusations, the hurled objects, the slammed doors and the tears. He'd always believed being an artist, a creator, was his raison d'être, his career, his calling. But life had turned out differently.

Soon after Leila had moved in, they had fallen into a brief relationship. Soon after that she'd told him she was pregnant. And his world had changed. He'd got a sensible job with a steady pay cheque but he had kept sculpting in his spare time. Happiness had fed his creativity. He and Leila had decided not to continue any form of romantic relationship, had wanted to focus instead on being parents, but they had remained living together so Marco could help, be part of the journey. Leo had been born and Marco had loved every minute; for six wonderful months he had been a hands-on dad, filled with love and pride in his beautiful, adorable little boy.

Then Leila had dropped her bombshell and his world had exploded and all his creativity had dried up. As if it had never been. He'd gone to his studio and it had all seemed so pointless. Things he'd made when he'd been deluded, when he'd believed himself to be a father, now looked tawdry, fake, rubbish. And he'd destroyed them all.

Leila had moved with Leo and Leo's real father to Australia and, left behind in the now, oh, so silent flat, Marco had felt his loss crystallise into a hardness, had realised that all his creativity had gone for good, buried in the avalanche of bleakness, loss and betrayal. So, to keep sane, to keep going, he had determined to succeed in a different way. A way he could control, a way that made sense, could be measured in cold, hard currency. Instead of iron, he'd forged a global business and become a tech billionaire.

'I set up a company instead. I am a businessman.' He looked at her closely; it seemed clear that she had no idea who he was. True, he wasn't an instantly recognisable figure, his only brush with celebrity a brief relationship with a supermodel three years before. Since their split he'd kept a low profile, had no need or desire to court celebrity status or public recognition.

'You really don't sculpt any more?' Her voice sounded shocked. 'You were so…focused, so passionate about it and so talented. Your ideas, your sketches, the pieces you showed me.'

'That was then,' he said shortly. 'I was young. It turns out I am better suited to business.'

'What sort of business is it?' she asked.

'Sales,' he said. There was a silence and her frown deepened.

'What sort of sales?' Her dark blue eyes focused on him. And then she blinked. 'It's okay. You don't need to tell me. I know. You set up a company, an online platform for people to sell things. You're Marco Stewart, aren't you? I should have recognised you. You are the founder and CEO of Krafty.'

'Yes.' He wondered why he hadn't wanted her to know. Perhaps it had simply been a tit-for-tat response or perhaps he had wanted her to remember him as he had been, an idealistic dreamer who'd been dedicated to art. Ridiculous. Idealism and dreams had taken him to heartache and misery. Being a businessman had brought him success, status and wealth. 'I am. You look surprised.' But she looked more than that, she looked a bit edgy, glanced round as if checking to see if anyone was watching them. Relaxed slightly when she saw no one was.

'Of course I am surprised. It's quite unusual to discover the first…someone you knew briefly years ago has become a billionaire businessman.'

'To be fair, it surprised me. I knew from experience how hard it is to sell your own products. So, I decided to set up an online community, an online marketplace for small businesses and entrepreneurs. It started out being for artists but I've expanded it now, to offer other goods and services. The whole thing took off.' Krafty was now a global phenomenon.

'So you don't sculpt any more? At all?' It was clear that she was having a hard time coming to terms with the idea and he felt his arms cross his chest in a gesture he recognised as defensive. Why, when he had nothing to defend? He'd made billions.

'There's no point. People would want to buy my work because of who I am, not the work itself.' There was truth in that even if it wasn't the whole truth. Again, her dark blue eyes looked into his and just like seven years ago he felt as though she could read his soul.

The idea set him further on edge. 'I'm not the person you knew briefly all those years ago.'

'No,' she said, and he heard a near sadness in her voice. 'Of course you aren't. You've moved on. That's why I didn't recognise you; I mean, I've read the odd article about Marco Stewart, billionaire entrepreneur, at various red-carpet events, but it never occurred to me that Marco Stewart could be my Marco from all those years ago. I always imagined you as a sculptor, the same long-haired dreamer you were then.'

'So, you imagined me?' he asked.

She bit her lip in clear annoyance, then shrugged. 'Of course I did, you helped me, you looked out for me, of course I remembered you sometimes, wondered how you were, how your life had panned out. Now I know.'

'And what about you?' he asked. 'How have the past seven years treated you?'

Her gaze wavered, went down to the now empty plates, and she lifted a finger and began to move the remaining crumbs into a little pile. 'I'm afraid I can't present any comparable achievements.' She glanced up. 'But I intend to change that.' Now her voice was steely, the tilt of her chin defiant.

'Is that why you're here?' he asked.

'Yes.' But he could hear a waver of doubt

now, as if reality was vying with the scale of her determination. But before he could question further, her phone beeped.

'Sorry. I'll need to have a look. It's my sister,' she explained.

'No problem. The same sister who loves gardens?'

Surprise flashed across her eyes as she looked at him, nodded and then looked down at her messages.

Her face paled as she inhaled sharply, and instinctively Marco leant forward in concern. She looked round the café, scanned the crowded streets and then pushed her chair back in an abrupt movement, rose to her feet and swivelled as if to flee. Recalling herself, she turned back. 'I have to go.' Her voice slightly breathless, though she managed to pull a smile to her face. 'I'm really glad you have done so well, but I have to run.'

She stretched out a hand and on automatic he rose, put his own hand out and as he clasped her fingers something shot through him. Desire sparked and buzzed but it was more than that. Her touch ignited memories. The first time he'd seen her, facing down a crowd of adolescents, her body poised for flight, her blue eyes wide with fear as she'd slowly backed away.

Back then she'd been a stranger in the city with no more than the clothes on her back.

As her gaze met his now, as he looked down at their clasped hands, Marco suspected that not a whole lot had changed. Tried to tell himself he was imagining it, that this was a simple case of trying to recapture something from his past, a misplaced moment of nostalgia. That he should let her go. But almost against his will he retained her hand in his. Knew he couldn't do that. Seven years ago, he'd betrayed her trust by kissing her and she'd left. He couldn't let her walk away into the unknown, into potential danger, again. Perhaps he was overreacting, but he had to know.

'Are you in trouble?' he asked.

CHAPTER THREE

Sofia stared down at their linked hands as sensations zigged and zagged through her, a mistimed, unwanted raw zing of attraction. She closed her eyes, told herself she was just mixed up. This was panic engendered by her sister's message, nothing to do with Marco.

The message on repeat in her brain

Dearest Sofia. You must take care. Father wants you to come back. The prince still wants to marry you. I think they have sent people to get you. I am so very glad I don't know where you are. Belle

At least she knew the message was authentic, the signature proved that. She and Rosa had agreed a code. Rosa would sign herself as Belle, not Rosa or Bella or Rosabella and that way Sofia would know the message was from her. As an additional precaution Rosa would use the phrase 'so very' in all her messages.

That meant the palace guards were looking for her. Most likely en route to Naples. Her father wasn't a fool. If he had decided to rescind the banishment, he would send people to the place he'd found her before.

So now was not the time to stand here staring down at a pair of linked hands, or to worry about what that touch was doing to her. She had to answer Marco's question in the negative. And leave. No way could she let him get mixed up in this whole mess. Not again.

'Are you in trouble?' he asked again, her hand still in his, that tug of awareness still shimmering a connection, igniting a spark in her tummy.

'No.'

'Is that a no you are not in trouble or a no you don't trust me enough to tell me? I'm sorry I betrayed that trust seven years ago. You can trust me now.'

Sofia frowned, wondered what Marco meant, saw genuine contrition in his grey eyes as he released her hand and she tried to ignore the foolish sense of being bereft. 'What do you mean? How did you betray my trust?'

'Seven years ago, I kissed you, and made

you feel you weren't safe with me. I drove you away.'

'No!' This time the denial was completely true, the syllable wrenched from her. 'How could you think that?' When the kiss had felt like the very best thing that had ever happened to her. A kiss that had awoken something in her, dizzied her, turned her knees to jelly, had filled her with glorious, wonderful sensations and a desire for more. That night she'd gone to sleep with a smile on her face, and dreams in her heart. The kiss was still one of her most treasured memories.

But Marco believed that the kiss had triggered her departure, that he'd done something wrong, scared her away. Sofia felt a pang of regret, of guilt that he had believed that for all these years.

'Our kiss…it had nothing to do with me going. I promise. That is the truth.' For a moment her own predicament was forgotten in the need to get him to believe that. 'That kiss…' Now, as if of their own volition, her feet moved her closer to him, she put a hand on his arm and froze, would swear a current was flowing between them as her fingers felt the sculpted muscle. 'That kiss was magical.' Now somehow her other hand was reaching up to touch his cheek and it felt as though time somersaulted, somehow fusing past and present, the Sofia and Marco of yesteryear and today. 'It didn't scare me or drive me away and it didn't betray trust. I trusted you implicitly.'

'Then trust me now.' His voice was deep, the sincerity palpable and the strength and warmth of his body, his sheer proximity, dizzied and reassured her at the same time. 'If you are in trouble let me help.'

Sofia saw the intense focus in his eyes. Knew she couldn't lie to him after what he had just said. 'I am in trouble, but you can't help. This time I need to deal with it on my own.' Stand on her own two feet, not simply be a damsel in distress. 'I won't involve you.'

'Why not?'

'Because it's not fair on you.'

'Maybe you should let me make that decision.' He hesitated. 'When you left last time, I truly was terrified something had happened to you. I can't watch you walk away now knowing you are in trouble or danger. At least let me try to help.'

Sofia's mind whirled as she tried to decide what to do. The problem being she *was* a damsel in distress and, like it or not, fate had brought her to a knight in shining armour. One her father could not possibly suspect as being her ally. Right now, there was no one else. Seven years ago, her father had tracked her down with ease; it would be even easier this time because she hadn't really tried to hide her trail. After all, she'd been banished, for cripes' sake.

Thoughts followed one after the other: realistically the security guards would be in Naples within hours and she had to make a choice. Leaving Naples was the best option but she couldn't afford to do that and, anyway, where would she go? She gritted her teeth; she would not go back yet, not go back to have pressure exerted on her to do her duty, to marry a man in love with someone else, a man who had a responsibility to his unborn child.

A sudden anger filled her. What right had her father to demand this of her? Her whole life he had made it clear he regretted her very existence, that her blood was tainted, so tainted he didn't want it to poison the royal bloodline. Had never once treated her with kindness or civility, yet always expected her unquestioning obedience. Dammit, she would not be dragged back ignominiously. Not this time.

But surely it still wasn't right to embroil Marco in her mess. Plus, how did she know she could trust him? He himself had said he was not the man she'd known seven years ago and had she really even known that man? How could she trust someone on the basis of one week? A week seen from a nineteen-year-old's perspective, through a rose-coloured filter.

After all, she had used the same filter in her relationship with Eli and look what had happened. That pink-tinged vision had led her to the precipice of disaster, had led to betrayal and humiliation. Because Eli had not been the man she'd believed nor hoped him to be.

So how could she trust this man? When she knew her desire to stemmed from a shallow *physical* desire for him, or perhaps an even more foolish romantic desire for a chivalrous knight.

But what was the alternative?

As if sensing her indecision, he took her hands back in his. 'Why don't you tell me what is going on? Even if you don't want my practical help, perhaps I can at least give you some advice.'

The café door swung open and instinctively Sofia swung round as panic surged. A scenario flashed through her brain of the guards crashing in. But it was okay, simply a woman entering, pushing a stroller. But it underlined the fact that she had to get moving. She turned back to Marco, her decision made.

'Okay. If you are sure. But can we go and talk somewhere more private, somewhere

where we won't be spotted?' The last thing she needed was for someone to recognise either of them.

He nodded. 'We could go back to my hotel. I've been using it as a base to work from as well as a place to stay. If anyone even notices us, which I doubt, they will assume you are a business colleague.'

Sofia hesitated, then nodded. Once inside they could be sure not to be observed and her father's guards would not come looking for her in Marco Stewart's suite. That was all that mattered. Once there she could at least have some time to think. 'That works. Thank you.'

'Let's go.'

They left the café, retraced their steps and then emerged onto a narrow iconic street that she recognised as one of the main roads that originated from the ancient city millennia before. Even as her mind raced with her own predicament, she couldn't help but wonder what the people from back then would think of the present-day Naples, her eyes absorbing the piazzas, a spectacularly decorated fourteenth-century church, the palaces all interspersed with lively vibrant shops and bakeries, the air scented with both traffic fumes and the waft of pizza dough and sugar.

But all the while the question remained of

how much to tell Marco. She had to remember that this version of Marco was different. No longer a dreamer, no longer a sculptor; he was now a billionaire entrepreneur who rubbed shoulders with influencers and celebrities. If she shared her identity, it was possible he would share that secret.

They came to a halt in front of a hotel that stopped her in her tracks, the building steeped in history, a grand old house, with a sweep of balustrades and a majestic stone entrance, set in a tiled courtyard lush with potted palm trees and flower beds. 'It's beautiful.'

'It's a renovated aristocratic house,' Marco said. 'And a protected historic site. The inside is even better.'

Sofia understood what he meant as they entered the lobby. The furniture was sleek and modern, the floors wooden, the reception desk made of gleaming metal and glass. Yet the ceiling boasted an ancient fresco that was somehow complemented by the minimalist décor. Her interior-designer eye took in all the detail even as she realised the need not to linger, to gain the privacy of his suite.

To her relief the area was busy enough that it was easy to head to the lifts without much notice being taken of them, bar a cursory wave to the man behind the desk. Then, within minutes, they entered Marco's suite and once again her brain absorbed the décor. 'I love how they've renovated it,' she said, taking in the sleek curve of the kitchen bar and the state-of-the-art chrome refrigerator, one gleaming white wall contrasted with a wood-panelled wall and feature wall of unadorned brickwork. A half-open door showed a spa-themed bathroom. 'It's a fabulous mix of past and present, contemporary but with whispers of history interlaced through.'

It was also, she thought, a marker of how far Marco had come, from the cheap and cheerful student digs of seven years ago to this boutique exclusiveness. It emphasised the changes in him, and increased her anxiety about how much she should trust him. 'Would you like another coffee?' Marco asked and she shook her head.

'No, thank you.'

They walked over to the glass-topped mahogany table by the large window and she caught her breath at the panoramic vista of Naples, the contrast between the narrow alleys and the iconic beauty of buildings dating back so many centuries. One last look and then she turned to face Marco, still not completely sure what she planned to say.

A deep breath and a last moment to filter

her words. 'There is something I would like to accomplish. A personal thing and Naples is where I can make a start.' Had already made a start; she'd tracked down the address of a potential relative of her mother's. 'However, for various complicated reasons my…family would prefer it if I go home. Much the same as seven years ago, they are going to send someone to take me back.'

There was a silence. 'By force?' His voice held an edge of anger. 'Is that what happened back then?'

'It's not that straightforward.' Her father's security guards had tracked her down and given her no choice, but, equally, 'Seven years ago I didn't resist.'

'Why not? Why didn't you call out? I could have helped.'

'I couldn't. It was important that no one knew about you.' She'd been scared what her father, what the guards, might do if they discovered Princess Sofia was sharing a house with a male, completely unchaperoned. Knew it sounded ridiculous in this day and age, but Palosian royalty hadn't moved with the times, her father determined to keep his family in a time warp. Now she was transported to seven years before. The sound of the windowpane slowly edging up, opening her eyes and feeling a frisson of fear. Her mouth open to scream for Marco. Then the figure at her bedside, the low voice—'Your Highness'—the recognition of a member of her father's palace guard. From then all her fear had been for Marco. And perhaps it was the memory, the vestige of her fear, that made her reach out now, to touch his hand.

An instinct she regretted as the touch ignited a fizz of something unfamiliar, a need, an urge to leave her hand where it was or better yet to trace the swell of his forearm, to feel the muscle under her fingers, to… Oh Lord, she had to get a grip. She took a deep breath and removed her hand. 'I know this sounds melodramatic, but it was for your own safety.'

She ran the words in her head, could hear how improbable they sounded.

'So you didn't call out, you didn't resist, you went with them to protect me?' Marco's voice held way more outrage than gratitude.

'Yes. But there is more to it than that. There was no point resisting. I always understood I had to go home at some point; I wasn't running away for ever.' Her place, as a Palosian princess, was in Palosia. She had duties and responsibilities. But, more than that, she would never leave Rosa. 'When they found me, I accepted the inevitability of having to return before I was ready to.'

'And when you got home?' he asked. 'What happened then?'

'Nothing. No one hurt me or harmed me.' Or not in the way he might be imagining. She had been assigned extra security, exposed to the invective of her father and then life had continued as normal, only with even more restrictions in place. A life where her father continued to grieve the fact he had no son to succeed him, so tried to consign his daughters to a non-life, as if by doing so he could forget their very existence. In truth, nothing very much *had* happened in seven years.

'I don't understand why you didn't get in touch. Let me know you were okay.'

'How?' she asked simply. 'I didn't even know your surname. I didn't have your phone number.'

'You could have written a letter to my address.'

It was a fair point. 'I couldn't.' If she'd written there was a chance he would have worked out who she was, however hard she tried to hide it. And how could she have explained anyway? 'I'm sorry. Truly I am. Somehow, once I got home, my time in Naples…it started to feel like a dream.' A treasured dream rather than a memory. The time they'd spent together, the kiss they'd shared that had meant so much to her, a sheltered princess. It had all been so incredibly magical she'd wanted to keep it as a dream, untouched by reality. Because she'd known it couldn't mean the same to Marco. To him a kiss was just a kiss, one of hundreds he'd have shared before and since. 'I'm sorry,' she repeated. Took a deep breath. 'But here and now I am worried the same thing will happen again and this time… This time I want to at least buy some time so that I can achieve something.'

The idea that so little had changed was dispiriting, sent a wave of frustration over her. Seven years later and she was still buffeted at the whim of her father's wishes, constrained and hedged by duty and royal protocol. Banishment had given her hope, the possibility of escape. That window was now slowly closing.

She wouldn't let it, not yet.

She became aware that Marco was studying her face. 'Maybe I can help,' he said.

Hope warred with pride. She truly wanted to stand on her own two feet. But, more than that, she wanted to find her mother, wanted to evade detection for at least a little longer, didn't want to be dragged back at her father's decree. 'How?' she asked.

CHAPTER FOUR

MARCO WONDERED IF he'd lost his mind; Sonia's story had so many holes he could drain pasta with it. It was a tale of melodrama and intrigue. People creeping in by night, a twenty-six-year-old woman unable to leave home, a chance reunion outside an estate agency.

The thought snagged. Was it chance? He had no idea who this woman was. Further doubts unravelled, warning him that he was perhaps being a fool. He more than anyone knew how easy it was to be led astray, conned, duped—for all he knew, Sonia had discovered that the man she'd once walked out on was now a billionaire, a man of wealth and means. It could be that it was no coincidence that she had been standing outside that estate agency. This could be a trap.

Logically that was more likely than her story being truth.

And yet…and yet…*surely*, he had seen genuine panic and fear in Sonia's dark blue eyes when the message had pinged through on her phone, seen sadness, frustration and heard resignation in her tone as she'd told her story. Enough to trigger a protective urge, a desire to help. Or was he being played, governed by attraction? Yet another unwelcome thought.

Because seven years on and the attraction between them was still there, only now he was more able to recognise it for what it was. Back then he'd had half-baked notions of romance and chivalry. But even in his youth he'd known the folly of both, had known that romance didn't last and when it sloughed away it left behind bitterness and regrets. Had seen that in his parents' marriage. And since then, he'd learnt another lesson. That even without the flowery veneer of romance, your world could be tipped from happiness to bleak disbelief and despair by the stark betrayal of trust. Had learnt of the duplicity of which people were capable. So *logically* the best thing to do was not get involved, to trust no one except himself.

But now, for the first time since Leila's betrayal, that principle was being tested. All because of a blast from the past, a time when he'd been more idealistic, more naïve. He studied Sonia's face, the wide blue eyes, the sign of strain and the still indomitable tilt of her chin, and he made up his mind.

He'd accept the chance he was being played, trust his instinct against the force of logic one last time; he'd go into this eyes wide open and keep his distance. Because he couldn't risk that she was telling the truth, that she was in trouble, however far-fetched it sounded. So, he'd help, but he would not get sucked into her orbit, would ignore the pull of attraction. He would not get emotionally or physically involved.

Realising the silence had stretched, he leant forward. 'You said you need to buy time. How did they find you last time?'

'I don't know. They worked out that I was in Naples and I think they literally combed the area; they must have got lucky and spotted me. That or there is a possibility my phone was tracked. I wasn't very good at covering my trail. This time I got a new phone when I arrived here and got rid of my old one. Only my sister has my new number. And she has a new phone as well.'

'Then what you need now is a place to hide out for a week or so. I imagine after that they will assume you aren't in Naples and move on to somewhere else?'

'I hope so,' she agreed. 'But a hotel is too visible and renting somewhere is…expensive and also requires some sort of identity and a bank account.'

He nodded. 'That's where I can help. You can stay in one of my properties. The villa I picked up the keys for earlier. No one will look for you there, or be able to trace you. It isn't even a rental property.' It was the perfect solution; he would take her there, make sure she had provisions and leave her there. If she was in trouble, it was the perfect bolt-hole. If she was a con artist, the most she would get out of him was a week's free accommodation and a grocery shop. He could check in with her daily, but there would be no danger of involvement. 'What do you think?'

Her face lit up. 'Are you sure? Won't that be inconvenient? Don't you need it?'

'No. I bought it as a holiday home for the family.'

'Family?' Her body tensed and she glanced round the suite. 'I didn't realise you were married. That changes everything. I can't expect you to help me if you have a wife, children...'

The words touched a nerve and he forced his body to stay relaxed; he had no child and he'd come to terms with it as much as it was possible to do so. No longer dreamt of Leo, no longer thought of him every day. Though the dull ache of loss remained, prodded into a flaring sear of pain by triggers that were unavoidable. The glimpse of a dark-haired baby boy, an innocent comment like Sonia's.

'I'm not married,' he said tersely. 'I bought the villa as a holiday home, primarily for my mother.' And her new family. He'd get something different for his father, a lodge in Scotland, a second home in the country Alec Stewart had missed so much and where he was happy now. 'She doesn't even know about it as yet. I'll tell her once it's redecorated. It is habitable now but it needs work and it's yours if you want it.'

'Thank you.' She folded her arms and he sensed her discomfort. 'I promise I will repay you one day; I can't pay much now but…'

He'd swear there was sincerity in her voice even as he told himself it could be fake. 'No need. It would be empty anyway. I'm not losing out.'

'Still, this time I will repay you.'

This time. The tacit acknowledgement of how things had changed. Seven years before neither of them had considered money or payment; their feelings, the sheer joy of spending time together, had transcended practicalities.

'Would it be possible to take me there now?' she asked. 'Or if you are happy to give me the keys, I can make my own way there.'

He glanced out of the window where dusk was throwing a gentle blanket over the sky-line. 'We can, but it may be better to go in the morning. The villa is on Capri. We'll need to cross by boat.'

'Capri?'

'Yes. Is that a problem?'

'No…or at least…' She shook her head. 'It's just I won't be able to get to work.'

'Where are you working?'

'It's a cleaning job. In an office. A few hours a night. I enjoy it; it's good to…have found something. I don't like letting the agency down at such short notice.' She shook her head, and gave a quick smile. 'Sorry. That is not your problem. I'll call now and then I'll get out of your hair. If we could go first thing in the morning that would be great.'

He watched as she pulled her phone out and dialled and curiosity surfaced. Her clothes would be impossible to afford on a cleaner's salary, the long-sleeved blouse and skirt plain but well cut. He wondered what her usual job was. Thought back to their time together; she'd never spoken much about her own hopes and dreams, just listened to him spout on about his visions of becoming a great sculptor.

His thoughts were distracted as her expression changed and he heard the volubility of the person on the other side.

'I understand,' she said. 'And thank you. I appreciate it. No. Yes. Of course.'

She dropped her phone into her pocket, her face once again leached of colour. 'They're here,' she said. 'That was Maria. The agency lady. She said someone contacted her, asking about any recent new employees.'

'That doesn't necessarily mean it is the people who are after you. It could have been a survey, or something to do with tax, or a clampdown on giving jobs to people without identity or...'

'Or it could have been the...the people who are looking for me. It's not a risk I can take.' He could hear the tremble in her voice, the vibe of panic, and a protective urge touched him. 'But how did they know to target cleaning agencies? Unless...' She grabbed her phone again and quickly typed a message.

A second later the phone buzzed and she looked down, before dropping the phone.

'What's wrong?'

'They have found my sister's phone. That's how they worked out to contact agencies. I told her I'd got a cleaning job.'

'But how can you know?'

'We have a code. I just messaged her; I got a message back but it's not from her.'

She took a deep breath and rose to her feet. 'I don't know if they are already in Naples or not. Is there any way you could give me the keys and I'll manage? I assume I can go by ferry if they're still running?'

Marco rose too. Perhaps he should let her go. But there it was again, a glimpse of the young woman she'd once been. Fear in her eyes that she was determined to conceal, defiance in the tilt of her chin as she pulled a smile to her face and, in that moment, he knew he couldn't let her walk out of here into unknown danger. *If* there were people out there looking for her it wasn't beyond the realms of possibility they would find her on the way to the ferry. What then? What if she walked out of here and he didn't see her again?

'I'll take you today,' he said. 'I can charter a private boat.'

Her forehead creased. 'Would you mind if we did get the ferry?' A hesitation and then she continued. 'You're a well-known person. If you charter a boat, it may garner attention and when you get on the boat with me some-one may question who I am.'

'That's fine. But we'll only just make the

last ferry. You won't have time to go back to the hotel.'

Sonia shook her head. 'I don't want to take the risk anyway. I've got my passport and a few bits and pieces with me. I'll call the hotel tomorrow and ask them to keep the rest of my things.'

'Then let's go,' Marco said, with a glance at his watch. 'Give me a minute to pack some things. I'll stay on Capri tonight. In case there are any problems.'

'In the villa?' She blinked. 'Of course you'll stay in the villa. It's yours. But…' She stepped backwards and now her eyes narrowed with sudden ware and he sensed an awkwardness as she cleared her throat. 'I'd better make something completely clear. I know what I said earlier about our… About our kiss. That was all true, but it doesn't mean I want to pick up from there; it was a long time ago and we are both different people now.'

Marco exhaled. Marvellous. Whilst he was busy suspecting her of ulterior motives, she was doing exactly the same and he supposed he couldn't blame her. 'Understood,' he said. 'And agreed. But one thing hasn't changed. You could trust me seven years ago not to cross the line and do anything you didn't want. The same holds good now. There are no strings attached here. At all.' Quite the contrary, in fact. 'But I was planning on staying in a hotel.'

'Oh.' For a second he wondered if there was a hint of disappointment in her face. If so, it vanished so fast he couldn't be sure. 'Thank you.'

'No problem. I'll be ready asap.'

Half an hour later they reached the ferry port and Sofia tried to quell the urge to look furtive, to dart sideways glances at every person. Perhaps this wasn't a good idea: if they had worked out that she knew Rosa's phone had been rumbled, they might be expecting her to leave Naples.

She found herself shifting closer to Marco's reassuring bulk. Reminded herself that she couldn't rely on his presence. She was still annoyed with herself for her assumption he would stay in the villa, even more annoyed at the fleeting sense of regret that he wasn't.

Relief touched her as she saw the ferry was ready to board and they stepped forward and merged with the others all making the same trip.

Once on board she relaxed slightly, looked out at the calm blue water and tried to breathe naturally. Focused on the man standing beside her; his warmth, the strength in his face, and she vowed that she'd pay him back. Somehow.

'Would you like something to eat? There's a snack bar through there,' he asked.

She turned to answer him and froze, saw a man walking through the ferry, looking around him. Surely that was one of the palace guards, scanning each section of the room, and in a minute, less than a minute, he'd see her.

'What's wrong?'

'There's…he…a guard…' He was going to see her, any second now. Running would draw attention. What could she do? Hell, she wasn't even sure it was a palace guard, he was obscured by the other passengers and she'd only caught a glimpse, couldn't risk looking more closely. But *if* it was…if he saw her… *Think*. He'd be looking for a woman on her own… Her brain leapt an intuitive leap.

'Sorry,' she muttered and before Marco could respond she moved so she was facing him, his body shielding her from view, stood on tiptoe and brushed her lips against his.

And that was all she'd meant to do, to stay frozen in pose until the guard moved on. But somehow as her lips touched his, as his lips touched hers, all the seething, simmering awareness of the past hours simmered over. His hands clasped her waist, her hands snaked up around his neck and then he was kissing her, she was kissing him.

Sofia's world seemed to tip on its axis. His lips felt… Both familiar and unfamiliar. Familiar because she'd revisited their kiss in her dreams, in treasured waking moments, and unfamiliar because this kiss was different. This kiss started out almost perfunctory and then something changed as she tasted the hint of pistachio, the tang of lemon, the sensation of his lips against hers and all thought seemed to float away and she was caught up in every heightened sense, lost to where she was, who she was, why she was, lost to everything but the spin of desire, his hand in her hair now as he deepened the kiss, and she pressed her body against his, wanting more, to be closer, nearer…wanting something she couldn't define. Her whole being consumed with want, need, greed, desire.

And then the ferry lurched slightly and the rocking motion brought some sort of reality back into focus, a reminder of where she was. Marco stepped back, one hand on her arm to steady her. His grey eyes were dark and she could see shell shock in them, succeeded by surprise and, she would swear, a flash of anger, though who it was directed at she couldn't be sure. She exhorted her brain to work, to think, to cut through the fugue of desire that still hazed it. 'I'm sorry,' she said. 'I thought I saw someone looking for me.' Carefully she shifted so that she could scan the room as discreetly as possible. 'I can't see him any more.'

Marco stepped back, his body still shielding her as he studied her expression searchingly, his grey eyes hard now, and she met his gaze head-on.

'I figured he wouldn't be looking for a couple so it seemed sensible to act like one. It was a spur-of-the-moment decision, and I apologise.' Though she wasn't sure if she was sorry. How could she regret a moment that had awoken such glorious sensations inside her? Caught in that bubble of desire, everything else had faded to insignificance.

But now…as she saw the grim set to the lips she'd just kissed so recklessly reality dawned—she'd kissed a virtual stranger with an abandon that sent a sudden wave of discomfort over her, a wave that doused the adrenalin, the sense of wonder, the heat of desire. Surely she hadn't imagined the fact that Marco had kissed her too; it hadn't all been one-sided. Had it? Doubts began to converge and she pushed them away, would deal with them later. Right now, she had to figure out how to avoid being taken back to Palosia.

'As I said, I apologise, but it seemed like a good idea at the time.' Now anxiety started to gnaw. 'If there is someone on the ferry looking for me, I have a problem. How much longer until we get to Capri?'

'About twenty minutes.'

'Okay. I need to make sure I'm not spotted if he makes his way back through here, or when we disembark.' She forced herself to meet his gaze. 'Would you mind continuing the couple pretence? Until we get to the villa? If we stay close, hopefully he won't spot me.'

'Sure.' His tone was even but something about the set of his jaw, the hard light in his grey eyes, set her on edge. Perhaps he was regretting this whole escapade and his offer of help, perhaps the kiss that had set her alight with yearning had had the opposite effect on him. 'What did this guy look like?' he asked.

'He's dark-haired, about five feet eleven and he was dressed in jeans, T-shirt and a lightweight tan-coloured jacket. I realise that is a bit generic. But he's also quite clearly scanning people.'

'I'll keep an eye out for him. But I suggest we assume he's watching when we disembark, so we try to get lost in the crowd, and walk out close together. Usually, I'd hire a car but that's not possible on the island. So maybe we'd better walk to the villa rather than get a taxi. Just in case he is enterprising enough to ask taxi drivers if they picked up a fare with a dark-haired woman, or shows your photograph at the taxi rank or bus stop.'

Surely there was something in his voice, almost as if…as if he was humouring her.

'That works,' she said evenly.

CHAPTER FIVE

MARCO GLANCED SIDEWAYS at Sonia as they disembarked and then scanned the area to see
if he really could see any suspicious-looking
character lurking. Tried to decide what the hell
was going on, but it was difficult when his
whole body was still reeling from the after-
effects of a kiss that had blindsided him, made
it difficult to decide which way was up, let
alone anything else. What had happened to the
'not get involved' policy? To the decision to ignore the attraction, and not allow it any scope?

Clearly it had been jettisoned. Because when
she'd brushed her lips against his, instinct had
taken over, and not a vestige of policy considerations had so much as crossed his mind. The
glorious sensations evoked by her lips, the feel
of her body pressed against his and he'd deepened the kiss, and then the sheer intoxication
of her response had meant that all that mattered

was the moment, the taste of her, the raw, visceral force of desire.

But as they exited the ferry, he could kick himself, knew he could not let himself be influenced by that kiss. A kiss that could have been a gambit taken from the cheesiest of films, a device to engineer a kiss, to mess with his head and distract him from the sheer improbability of her story. Codes and phone trackers and suspicious stalkers. It could all be designed to gain access to a billionaire.

Yet he scanned the crowd looking for the man Sonia had described and they both saw him at the same time. He instinctively moved to shield her from the man's line of view, but his quick glance showed him that the dark-haired man was talking with a crew member, gesticulating urgently as he spoke.

Could Sonia be telling the truth?

'Was that him?' he asked and she nodded, her stride increasing.

'Slow down. You're more likely to catch his eye if you don't act normally.'

'Is it far to the villa?' Her voice urgent.

'About a thirty-minute walk,' he said.

For a while they walked in silence, past the whitewashed buildings, shops and restaurants, up the narrow winding roads that characterised the small cliff-laden island and meant there was very little traffic other than the elongated vintage taxis or the almost miniature orange buses that glided by at irregular intervals. Each one scanned by Sonia's anxious eyes and he sensed the tension in her body, had to counter the urge to step closer to her, to offer reassurance. Tried to remind himself there was a chance she was simply acting. How could he tell? He'd had no clue that Leila had been playing him from the first. Had been suckered in, clueless from start to finish. The memory hardened his resolve, his stride increasing slightly even as he tried to focus on the warming sun, the tangy citrus smell of lemons, the bright stretches of flowers that scented the Mediterranean air.

Yet the idea that he could be being played persisted, caused an edginess he couldn't shake. The sense heightened by the sheer rawness of the desire that still seethed inside him, making it impossible to view Sonia with any clarity. His judgement clouded, making him easy prey if she was indeed trying to pull his strings. The idea he was dancing to her tune, the idea that by kissing her he'd ceded control of his own objectivity, galled him, caused his lips to set in a grim line, and he was aware of her sideways glance.

'Can I ask you something?' she said.

'Sure.'

'Why are you helping me?' she blurted out.

Perhaps he should have thought before he spoke, worded his answer better, but he couldn't, wanted her to know, wanted to remind himself that he wasn't utterly clueless now.

'Because you've claimed you're in trouble and I can't take the risk that you're telling the truth.'

'Excuse me?' There was anger in her voice, but there was hurt as well. 'What risk? Are you saying you are doubting my word?'

Marco considered his options and decided that perhaps the truth was the best way to go. Call this out here and now. 'It is hard to know what to believe when you won't even tell me your real name.' He could hear the derision in his tone. 'The story you've told me; it sounds like something from a soap opera.'

'But why would I make it up?'

He shrugged. 'You wouldn't be the first to target a billionaire with a story designed to elicit sympathy.' That was the truth. Leila hadn't been targeting wealth, she had wanted a father for her baby. But since his material and business success Marco had been shocked by the number of accidental meetings and overtures that had been extended to him.

Sonia slammed to a stop beside him and ire flashed from her eyes. 'You think… Oh my God…you think I've orchestrated everything, including what happened on the ferry. You think I'm trying to seduce you?'

Outrage dripped from every word and anger vibrated from her.

'Well, think again,' she said. 'Every word I have told you is the truth; I have no interest in your money. I have no interest in you. So, thank you for your offer of help but you can stuff it. I'll take my chances on my own.'

With that she spun on her heel and started walking, leaving Marco looking after her, his head reeling.

What the hell was wrong with him? He'd made a decision to offer help, and now, because he had messed up and kissed her *again*, he had goaded her into walking away. Bottom line was there was a chance she was in trouble. The guy at the ferry had been suspicious, Sonia *had* vanished without trace all those years ago, and, dammit, there had been the ring of truth in every word she'd said. He wasn't letting her disappear again, not this time.

'Wait,' he called, hastening after her when she didn't so much as break stride.

He strode after her, caught up and placed a

hand on her arm, ignored her efforts to shake it off.

'Listen to me. You can't take your chances. You know that. If you are telling the truth, if that man was after you, you are walking straight back into his arms. Seven years ago, you said you went with them to protect me. Well, now it's my turn to protect you. If I don't and you disappear again, I'll have years more of regret on my conscience and this time the regrets would be justified. So, my offer of the villa still stands. Don't pass that up because I have a few legitimate doubts about your story.'

Her pace slowed and she glared down at his hand. Stepping back, he removed it.

'Surely I am entitled to have doubts? In the past two years since I've made my money countless women have engineered "accidental" meetings with me, have tried to seduce me. Yes, it has made me wary. But that doesn't mean my offer of help isn't valid. Plus, you've made it clear you don't trust me either. You didn't seven years ago and you don't now.' He halted now. 'It's up to you.'

Up to her. Sofia tried to focus through the haze of righteous anger. Realised her anger stemmed from hurt. She'd felt safe with him, touched that he still wanted to protect her just as he had years before. Now it turned out that he thought she'd fabricated her plight as a ruse to target his wealth. That she'd kissed him as part of that ploy.

The idea was abhorrent, the whole scenario reminiscent of Eli. Eli, who had professed undying adoration, all because he had an eye to marrying royalty. Eli had kissed Sofia, cold-blooded kisses, part of a ploy. Now she wiped her mouth with the back of her hand and took a deep breath, actually thought about what Marco had said. Had to concede that maybe, just maybe, he had a point.

Quite a few points.

Her story did sound fantastical and he clearly had been targeted before for his wealth. But… she studied his expression now, and she sensed that there was more at play here, that something bigger had destroyed his ability to trust, that the shadows she had glimpsed in his grey eyes stemmed from baggage that was truly heavy.

And yet despite all that he'd still chosen to offer help, to give her the benefit of the doubt and a sudden sense of appreciation defused her anger.

She looked up and met his gaze.

'If the offer stands, I'll take it. Thank you.'

To her surprise and perhaps to his, her reply

garnered a smile from him. A smile that still made her tummy give a funny little lurch of desire.

'I'm glad,' he said simply. 'Truce?' He held out a hand and for an instant she studied its shape and strength and goosebumps shivered her skin as she reached out and shook it.

'Truce,' she repeated and offered an answering smile, though she was quick to withdraw her hand. No way would she give him any reason, however tenuous, to suspect she was trying to seduce him, to give credence to the idea she was a gold-digger. So, as they walked, she was careful not to get too close.

Fifteen minutes later, Marco gestured. 'That's the one.'

Sofia stared at the sprawling elegant edifice, the tall arches and white plaster walls, set within a mosaicked courtyard surrounded by a stone wall, sectioned with Roman columns. She looked up at the roof of curved terracotta clay tiles and the jut of the balconied terrace, the whole thing another stark reminder of how wealthy Marco was if he could make a purchase like this as a holiday home for someone else. 'It's stunning,' she said, aware of an urge to sketch it to capture the Mediterranean architecture on the page.

A tiled pathway lined with colourful pots

containing shrubs led to a front door that made her come to a halt. The arched door made of heavy Venetian glass allowed a tantalising glimpse into the interior of the house. 'I've never seen anything like this.'

'It was one of the reasons I bought the house. Well, that and where it's located.' He opened the front door and stood back so she could enter. 'I can show you around straight away if you like?' he offered.

'I'd love that.' The interior designer in her was eager to look at the rooms, come up with ideas, even though she knew the exercise would be done solely for herself, aware of a wish Marco were bringing her here because she was a bona fide interior designer.

She followed him along an entrance tiled with what looked like original ceramic tiles, through to a living room and a reception room both sporting high vaulted ceilings, featuring gold leaf and wooden beams, and cool marble floors. Massive arched glass windows showcased a view of a garden where rose bushes and lemon trees abounded and the lounge boasted an immense glass door leading onto a large covered terrace.

'Your mum will love this. It's truly beautiful and has such potential.' She glanced at him and a pang assailed her as she tried to picture having a mother who had done so much for you that you wanted to give her a gift of such beauty.

'Thank you,' he said. 'I'll show you the rest of the house. There are four en suite bedrooms as well,' Marco explained. 'Two of them are furnished, though like in all the rooms the furniture is a bit basic, a hotchpotch of things the previous owner didn't want.' He took a deep breath. 'So, I thought I'd stay tonight. You can choose whichever room you prefer and I'll take the other.'

'Stay?' Sofia shook her head. 'No way.' Not whilst he doubted her story and her motivation, and would probably barricade his door. 'There is no need. I have everything I need here and if I do run into any problems I can contact you.'

'I disagree. If the man you saw is looking for you there is a chance he will knock on random villa doors; he could be lurking outside, could knock on the neighboring villas' doors and ask if anyone saw any strangers or new people. Hell, he may stay in the same hotel as me, recognise me from the ferry and ask where the woman I was with is. It is better if I stay here.'

'Even though you have doubts about my story?'

'Doubts that I accept may be misplaced. If I leave here tonight and I return tomorrow and you're gone I'll never know what happened, won't even know where you are. Whether you have simply decided to leave or whether you have been spirited away.'

The words made her pause. The possibility that Marco would never know for sure that she wasn't a con artist made her skin prickle with the sheer unacceptability of it. Or what if he stayed and the guards turned up and he got hurt trying to protect her when he didn't even know who he was protecting? The idea horrified her.

Yet she hesitated. If she revealed the truth, she was putting her future in his hands and all her previous doubts resurfaced. Her own dubious ability to judge men's trustworthiness, amply demonstrated by how she'd believed Eli, the fact she barely knew Marco and even *if* she had been able to trust him years before that didn't mean she could now. But more than that was the knowledge that if Marco did betray her that would devastate her, would shatter the memories she had held so close to her of their magical week together.

Instinct told her she could trust him, but she couldn't be certain that her doubts were unfounded. Maybe she should channel her sister. Rosa always believed the best of people; that was what Sofia would do now. Take the risk in the interest of doing what she knew to be right. She couldn't ask him to put himself in danger without knowing the facts.

'If you are going to stay then you need to know the truth. I *want* you to make that choice knowing the truth.'

'Are you sure?' His face held a serious expression, as if he understood that this wasn't a decision she'd made lightly.

'Yes.'

'Then let's go and sit on the terrace. It's still warm and the previous owner has left a bottle of wine and some food in the fridge. We can have a picnic on the terrace and talk.'

'That sounds good.'

'You go and sit. I'll bring everything.'

She nodded, stepped towards the glass doors that led onto the terrace and stood, mesmerised by the sweeping panoramic vista before her. The famous rock formations that had been shaped and weathered over millions of years, the peak and jut of cliff faces, the spread of whitewashed edifices and the glinting aquamarine ripple of the sea. The whole thing took her breath away and as she gazed out, she tried to decide the best way to explain who she was, knew that there was no way to build up to the revelation of her identity. Hoped she'd made the right decision to trust him.

CHAPTER SIX

MARCO HANDED SONIA a glass of cold sparkling wine, and sat opposite her on one of the cushioned chairs placed under the wicker-ceiled covering, made sure he kept his body relaxed, his expression neutral, not wanting to overwhelm her or force anything. This was clearly a big deal and he wouldn't rush her.

'I'm a princess,' she said simply. 'Her Royal Highness Princess Sofia of Palosia, to be exact.'

There was silence as he looked at her, his brain reeling, because whatever he might have suspected, this was not it. 'You're kidding, right?'

'Nope. It's the truth. I mean, Palosia isn't a massive country or anything but it's a monarchy with a royal family.' She reached down into her bag and pulled out her passport, and he took it. Even now, at this moment of shock, a frisson ruffled the air as his hand brushed hers. And he realised whatever else changed with her revelation, this hadn't, the attraction impervious to rank or status.

He opened the passport, looked down at the unfamiliar official stamp, the ornate lettering, the crystal-clear confirmation that the woman sitting opposite him was a royal princess. The idea difficult to wrap his brain round. The woman he'd rescued on the streets of Naples seven years before was a princess. For all these years he hadn't known something so massive. Thoughts and emotions collided: a wish she'd told him before, a sense of the surreal but most of all an overriding happiness that she wasn't playing him. This wasn't a scam or a con, Sonia, no, Sofia, was on the level.

Marco frowned, aware the happiness was out of proportion, told himself it was simple relief that he could now ask questions, make decisions without second-guessing. And now he did want to ask questions, know more, understand exactly what was happening.

He trawled his mind for what he knew about Palosia. Not very much, just a hazy memory of an article once perused.

'Palosia is an island, a small island, a monarchy, growing in economic importance, due to its recent export of specialist olive oil.' But that was all he knew; the article hadn't detailed members of the royal family.

She nodded. 'Yes. About twenty years ago we discovered a whole new olive variety that thrives in Palosian soil. It's kind of lemony and nutty and it's unique to us. It's put Palosia on the global map, or at least Europe's. It's a beautiful place,' she said, and he could hear the pride in her voice.

'But why are you here? Is there unrest on Palosia? Is that why you have left?' His brain whirled with the idea of royal intrigue, revolutionary uprisings.

Sofia shook her head. 'There is no unrest. My father is not a popular ruler personally but the people accept his rule, accept that it is fair and brings Palosia prosperity. I left because… my father banished me.' She gave a small smile, a smile that held a wealth of sadness, and instinctively he moved his chair closer to hers. 'Another twist in the soap-opera plot.'

'What happened?' he asked.

'On Palosia the rules for royalty are very traditional, the customs date back years. Even though the women on Palosia are moving towards more modern ideas, my father has chosen not to allow this at court. He insists royal princesses adhere to the old ways, has made no attempt to catch up with the twenty first century. Women can't inherit the throne.' He heard the catch of frustration in her voice, but also a note of bitterness, the shadows in her eyes deepening. 'And my father doesn't believe in princesses having careers; he believes our job is to be royal, to carry out royal duties at his decree. The main royal duty being to marry advantageously.'

'An arranged marriage?' Marco didn't even try to keep the surprise from his voice.

'Yes,' Sofia said. 'Such marriages have taken place in royal families since the dawn of time. Rosa and I have always known our fate is to marry for the good of Palosia.' She sipped her wine, picked up an olive and looked out at the sky that was deepening to a navy darkness, obscuring the jagged cliff lines, the waves of the sea silhouetted. 'I know how old-fashioned it sounds, but if you look back at my country's history so many marriages based on an alliance worked, endured. Maybe because the people were well matched, had the same backgrounds, goals and an understanding of what they expected from a marriage. I believe that can work, but for it to work there has to be trust and both parties have to agree there can be no regrets or yearning for love.'

Marco considered the words, could see the logic behind them. Look at his own parents:

love had turned bitter and that had meant they couldn't work out a way to coparent, to navigate a path to stay together in any sort of harmony. Or perhaps it had never been love, perhaps it had simply been attraction that had masked incompatibilities and in the end perhaps liking, having similar outlooks, did trump love or attraction.

'I thought about it long and hard and, in the end, I realised that marriage gave me so much. Freedom, a purpose and a chance to have a family. To bring up my children in security, in a peaceful atmosphere without drama. Love brings drama, it changes how you think, affects your decisions.' She sipped her wine. 'So, when my father arranged a marriage with a prince of a neighbouring island I agreed. And I would have married Eduardo, I was literally ready to go to the altar when…I discovered that Eduardo was in love with another woman. A woman who was in love with him. Whilst I knew our marriage was one of convenience, I couldn't marry a man who was in love with someone else. I pulled out of the wedding. My father banished me. Said I had let down my country, let down my people.'

'Is that what you believe?' He heard pain in her voice, an underlay of regret to the resolution, and his heart twisted as he moved his chair a little closer to hers, wanting to show solidarity.

'I don't think I could have made a different decision,' she said slowly. 'But yes, I do regret that it didn't work out as I expected. The trade deal my father made with Eduardo's father was very advantageous for both countries and the marriage was arranged to seal the deal. I wanted to do that for my country. And I understand that Eduardo wanted to do the right thing for his. According to my sister, he still does. That's why my father wants me to go back. Eduardo still wants to marry me.'

There was anxiety in her voice now and Marco felt a surge of protectiveness as he tried to understand her upbringing. 'But they can't force you,' he said. 'Can they?'

She shook her head. 'It isn't a question of forcing me; they can exert pressure. My father is ruthless where Palosia is concerned. He won't use physical coercion but he will use leverage. As Eduardo's father will. I had hoped, assumed, Eduardo would hold firm. But if he doesn't, I will. I can't marry a man who is in love with someone else. Not when he may regret it for the rest of his life, not when it may impact any children we would have.'

Marco picked up his phone and did a quick search. 'The only publicity around the wedding is a fairly brief piece saying that "It is understood from the palace that Princess Sofia was taken ill minutes before she was due to leave for the church. The family requests privacy at this difficult time. Prince Eduardo is understandably concerned and is believed to be by his fiancée's side.'"

Sofia nodded. 'They are buying time until they can find me.'

'Why doesn't your father simply ask you to come back?'

Her laugh was singularly mirthless. 'Because he doesn't work like that. He wouldn't deign to negotiate or ask. He believes I owe him complete obedience. But I hope the longer I stay away, the more likely it is that Eduardo will decide not to marry me. I would at least like to go back on my own terms.'

'To another arranged marriage?'

'Yes,' she said simply and he couldn't help his frown. 'Try not to judge.'

'I am not judging,' he said. 'I can see the sense in an arranged marriage, but I struggle with the idea of marriage full stop. And even in an arranged marriage, surely there is a risk that one of you will fall in love with someone else at some point? Eduardo could have met the woman he is in love with after you'd got married.'

'If he had, I hope that he would never have let it progress to the point of love, would have walked away at the first sign of danger. Marriage is my only real option. The only way I can have a family. As a Palosian princess, if I want children marriage is a prerequisite. And I do want children. In this type of marriage my children will have two parents who are committed to being loving parents, who aren't distracted by the drama of loving each other. I will provide stability, security and love for them.' Her voice was fierce with determination and he nodded acknowledgement.

'I get that. But...' He hesitated, aware that Sofia's upbringing, her culture, her country's traditions were important.

She gestured with her hand. 'It's okay. You can say whatever you are thinking.' Her lips upturned in a sudden smile, both genuine and sweet. 'It's nice to have a real conversation, to get someone else's take on things. I am very aware of how sheltered my life has been, so please go ahead.'

'I understand all the reasons on paper for you to accept an arranged marriage. Duty, family... But...what about the actual realities of marriage?' He might as well lay it on the line. 'What about attraction? Are you attracted to Eduardo?'

'Attraction is overrated,' she said flatly.

He raised his eyebrows. 'Are you sure?' he asked softly as a memory of the kiss they had shared just hours ago flooded his mind: the desire, her response to his touch. How could a woman as vital, as passionate as Sofia be willing to forgo attraction for the rest of her life? She had kissed him as though her life depended on it, a kiss that even now had his lips tingling. He looked at her and he couldn't help it, his gaze dropped to her lips and for an insane instant he wanted to kiss her again, *show* her the importance of attraction.

Heat touched her cheeks but she met his gaze full-on. 'I'm sure. Attraction messes with your head. It makes you make questionable decisions. Sparks cause fire.'

'Fire is a good thing. It creates warmth, gives pleasure.'

'Fires can burn out of control, cause hurt and devastation. I'll stick to central heating. Pleasure doesn't outweigh what is *really* important. Respect, liking, compatibility, those things make the bedrock of a marriage. I believed Eduardo to be a good man, with an understanding of how royalty works. He was even happy for me to pursue some sort of job.'

Marco wondered how it must feel to not be

allowed to pursue a career. 'If you could have any job, what would you do?' he asked.

Sofia didn't hesitate. 'I'd train as an interior designer. I did an online course a year ago and I loved it. Eduardo said I could renovate some of the royal residences. I hoped to use that experience to branch out, get a real job. That means more to me than any spark.'

She tipped her chin out as if daring him to challenge her further. A challenge he had no wish to take up because he could see her point of view, could understand that for a woman in her position the benefits of an arranged marriage far outweighed the disadvantages. As for attraction, she had a point. His own parents had mistaken physical compatibility for real compatibility.

'Anyway,' she said now, 'that's enough about me. I'm assuming from what you've said that you want it all. Sparks, love, the "real thing"?'

'God, no.'

Her eyebrows rose at the vehemence in his voice.

'Then what is your take on relationships?'

It was a fair question. After all, he'd given his opinion on her take. She was entitled to do the same. 'I'm not sure I have one; I do know that commitment doesn't work for me.' It wasn't as though he minded being on his own;

that was the safest way to be. Involvement led to complication and to pain.

'Why not?'

'Because whether it is based on an arrangement or love it doesn't come with a guarantee. Most people believe love conquers all, but love is not necessarily a long-lasting phenomenon; too many relationships break down and too many people race to the altar, floating on a delusional cloud of romance, and then real life kicks in and they realise romance isn't enough.'

She nodded. 'Or they race to the altar on a lava-hot floor of attraction. And that doesn't last either. The volcano stops and you're left with destruction.'

He grinned at her and raised his glass. 'To cynicism.'

'To realism,' she countered, before putting her glass down and looking at him thoughtfully. 'But where does that leave you? I mean, what about children?'

'Not for me.' His voice terse. No way would he risk that again. His own experience with his parents and his short time as Leo's father had shown him that parenthood held too many pitfalls, too many paths to pain and grief. Before Leo, he'd believed that if a relationship went wrong joint custody could work. He still believed that, but he could now see that even if joint custody was best for the child, it could be heartbreaking for a parent. Even if Leo had been his in the end there would have been loss and pain when Leila met someone else. Watching his son being brought up by another man. Helpless to do anything if Leila had taken Leo halfway across the world.

Aware that Sofia was looking at him, he blinked the thoughts away and shrugged. 'Because I don't believe in love lasting or any long-term relationship lasting. So, it's not fair to risk bringing a child into that. It's not really even fair to enter any relationship.'

'You did try though? I am sure I saw a few articles about you and a supermodel. Cynthia Martinez.'

'I did date Cynthia and that's why I know relationships don't work for me. Krafty had just taken off and I was being asked to a lot of celebrity events.' And he'd decided to embrace the jet-setting, super-rich lifestyle as a way of showing himself that he'd moved on from Leila's betrayal, from the loss of a son he'd never truly had. 'I met Cynthia at some sort of gala. She asked me to dinner and I accepted. I shouldn't have. Or at least I shouldn't have let it go any further.'

'Why not?'

'I knew it couldn't go anywhere. I was still

so caught up with work, with taking the company to the next step, I didn't have time for a relationship.' That had been his official line, the one he'd finally told Cynthia.

'But it was more than that,' Sofia said softly.

'Yes.' In truth he'd spent the whole relationship feeling guilty, because each date had seemed to emphasise the fact that he hadn't moved on. Exacerbated the knowledge that he'd trade this life of celebrity dating and wealth to have Leo back. For Leo to be his real son. And he'd realised it wasn't fair to use a relationship to prove anything. To use another human being. He wouldn't do that again.

'Relationships don't work for me, because I feel like a fraud. If I am going into it not wanting commitment or long-term, knowing it can go nowhere, then what's the point? What do I have to offer?'

Sofia looked at him for a long moment. 'Do you really want me to answer that?' she asked. And just like that the atmosphere shifted slightly.

'Yes. I do. Go ahead.'

CHAPTER SEVEN

FOR HEAVEN'S SAKE, what was she doing? Had the wine gone to her head? Nope, it wasn't that—she'd only had a glass and a half. It wasn't the wine. It was the company, the heady exhilaration of feeling safe, of having a real conversation. Like it or not, it was also the undercurrent, a current that was zinging as they spoke, as the night fell in around them. Now she looked up at the glittering pinpoints of starlight, felt the soft warm breeze, the night-lit illumination of Capri, and she knew that, this time, these moments were precious.

Not for Marco, but for her.

Because she'd painted her future for him, a destiny she'd always accepted as her fate, a future she *wanted*. It was her way to prove to her father, prove to herself, that she was truly a princess, understood her duty to her country. But she knew that future wouldn't include evenings like this, a place and time where her status was irrelevant, where desire shimmered in the air as bright as the starlight from above.

There was more than that: she'd seen the shadows in his eyes, and she wanted to lighten the mood, make him smile, make him… *Make him what, Sofia?* Kiss her again? This time for real, because he wanted to.

No. Attraction *was* overrated, sparks could cause devastation. But that didn't mean she couldn't indulge in a little flirtation; after all, she was a long way from home and Palosia's rules and etiquette.

And she was aware now that whilst she had been thinking she had also been studying him, and, somehow, she seemed to have shifted a little closer.

'Yes, I would like you to answer that,' he repeated. 'What *do* I have to offer?' His tone deep now, it shivered over her skin leaving a trail of goosebumps.

'Hm, well, let's see… You're…' deliberately now she let her eyes rove his face, let her gaze focus on his lips, and she felt her pulse rate ratchet '…pretty good-looking, you're young and…' Now her eyes dipped and lingered on the swell and breadth of his body. 'And you look like you're pretty fit, work out a lot.'

'You're saying I have stamina?' The low rumble of his voice held a note of banter and a deeper note of promise that triggered a stream of toe-curling images.

'I'm saying,' she managed, 'that you look good. You also have plenty of money to wine and dine a woman in style and pay your own way. As for your stamina, I'll have to take your word for it.'

'You have my word. I believe in stamina. And strength. And technique.'

Okay. She was getting way out of her depth here.

'Then you can put all that on the table too. The point I'm making...' What was the point she was making? It was difficult to know when he looked at her like this, his grey eyes dark with something that churned her up inside, her pulse rate now off the charts. 'The point I am making is...' She pulled herself together. Dammit, she would not let him see how he was affecting her. 'Why not be upfront with women and say you're looking for short term? I am sure there are women out there who don't want commitment either. Then you won't feel like a fraud. And you could enjoy a strings-free relationship. Just have fun.'

The idea sounded definitively appealing. And she gathered speed.

'There are so many things to do out there and you are free to do whatever you want whenever you want. I can't even imagine that.' As children she and Rosa had had some freedom, simply because their father hadn't cared what they were doing. But after Sofia's escape to Naples that had drastically changed. 'If I want to go for a walk, I have to tell someone where I'm going and most of the time if it isn't on palace grounds I have to take someone with me. Even on palace grounds there is always someone keeping an eye on me.'

She shrugged. 'You can get up and go for a walk anywhere. Hell, you can go for a run, a swim, catch a plane to anywhere in the world. Sightsee, visit historic sights, go out and eat pizza or whatever you like. And you can choose who you ask to do that with. You are free to ask any woman you like on a date, and I am sure there are plenty of women out there who would love to have some short-term fun. As long as you are honest with them it would work.'

For one sweeping instant she allowed her imagination full rein, imagined a different world where Marco and she were sitting here on this balcony because she was one of those women. That they were here to have fun, instead of here through necessity. But that was not possible. 'My choices are limited by who I am... Yours aren't.' She put her glass down on the table. 'So go out and have fun.' She stopped, aware that he hadn't said anything for a while. 'Sorry. I may have got a bit carried away there. It's just an idea.'

'No need to apologise. I appreciate the input.' His face serious now. 'When you said your life was full of restriction, I didn't realise the extent. Are princesses not allowed to date at all?'

'No.'

'So, you've never been out for dinner or to the movies with someone?'

'No.' She shrugged. 'But, much as I hate to admit it, there is a point to that rule. Another reason why I think an arranged marriage is best. I did have a relationship and it was a disaster. I met Eli at a court event, the annual summer dinner my father puts on for the aristocratic families.'

Sofia had always looked forward to these as a break in the monotony of their existence. It was also an occasion where, for appearances' sake, her father, the courtiers, had to show her at least some respect. Not that she would tell Marco this. She had no intention of moaning or complaining about the difficulties of her childhood. Those things were private. She would never risk confiding in anyone, couldn't bear to see the daily humiliations of her life made public.

'He was a couple of years older than me and the son of one of Palosia's leading families so it was okay for him to dance with me. We got talking and it was…nice.' In truth, she had been so starved of affection and attention that someone complimenting her had turned her head. Made her believe that maybe Eli was like Marco. That she could recapture, re-experience something of the feeling Marco had evoked. 'He asked if I'd meet him. He was a younger son so we knew it wouldn't be allowed officially, so we used to sneak meetings. It was risky but it made me feel alive.' And good about herself.

'What happened?'

She sighed. 'I realised he didn't really like me. I'd already suspected something wasn't right.' When he'd kissed her, she'd anticipated the same magic she had felt with Marco, she'd tried to instil the kisses with even a vestige of the dizzying sensations Marco had evoked. But they had just felt awkward. 'Then I saw a message on his phone one day. It was a friend asking if he'd managed to get any pictures. I asked him what it meant and in the end he confessed. He was hoping to get compromising pictures of me, and get me to fall for him and then use both those things as leverage to marry me. I was furious. With myself even more than him. I should have seen through him.'

'It's not always that simple,' Marco said and she could see understanding and surely a light of empathy in his eyes. 'A betrayal of trust of that magnitude is difficult to accept, makes you feel like a fool. But you weren't. Eli is the one who was at fault.'

'Thank you. But at least it taught me a valuable lesson. That men will want to marry me for who I am. In which case the best thing I can do is accept that and make sure that there is also something in it for me. An arranged marriage allows me to do that.'

'Not all men are like Eli,' he said.

'No,' she conceded. 'But realistically all the men I am destined to meet on Palosia, all the men my father would approve of, are going to want to marry me for my title. I have accepted that and I've realised that I can't expect attraction. With Eli... I thought kissing him would be like kissing you. I had a romantic belief that all kisses would be like the one I had shared with you. After Eli I knew that wasn't the case, that with the limited pool of eligible men magical kisses are unlikely to be part of the deal.' There was a silence and she jutted her chin out. 'I'm good with that. It works for me.'

He looked at her. 'For what it's worth, that kiss was magical for me as well.'

'You don't have to say that. I know you will have shared hundreds of other kisses.'

'Not like ours. I'll never share another kiss like that. It was my first kiss that meant anything. Even aged twenty-one I'd never believed in romance. You turned that on its head. That week with you I did believe that anything was possible; when I was with you nothing else mattered except you.'

The words were said with a depth of sincerity and the knowledge of their truth made her yearn to kiss him again, to relive the magic. But that wasn't possible. Seven years separated that moment from this and they were two different people now. Yet the temptation wouldn't cede; what harm could there be in one kiss?

Stop. What was she doing? Seven years ago, she'd let Marco and attraction and foolish ideas about romance mess with her head, distract her from her real purpose in being here. To find her mother. Not this time.

With a movement she recognised as abrupt she pushed her chair back, managed to pull a smile to her face. 'We seem to have wandered from the point. Now you know who I am, I understand if you would rather not stay.'

Marco blinked, ran a hand over his face

and then pushed his own chair back a little as though he too wished to emphasise the space between them. 'I'm staying,' he said. 'I am not leaving you here to be found by the palace guards. And, Sofia...?' The sound of her real name on his lips seemed to resonate through her. 'Thank you for trusting me. I will do all I can to keep you safe.'

The idea that there was someone on her side gave her a sense of strength, an optimism that maybe she could hold out against her father.

'Thank you.'

He rose to his feet. 'Now I'd better check we have all we need. I suggest you have the first bedroom and I'll have the second one.'

She nodded, told herself that history would not repeat. This time the guards would not silently appear in her room. As if reading her mind, he stepped towards her, reached out and lightly touched her forearm, the touch retriggering awareness. 'They have no reason to suspect that their princess is hiding out with me. No way of knowing that we know each other.'

He was right and she smiled at him. 'Thank you. For everything, Marco.'

'You're welcome. Now what we both need is a good night's sleep. Then tomorrow we can come up with a plan of action.'

CHAPTER EIGHT

PLAN OF ACTION. Marco opened his eyes, took in the dingy white of the ceiling that needed a coat of paint, sat straight up on the double bed that had seen better days. He'd slept sketchily the previous night, on high alert for suspicious sounds or intruders. But before he'd dropped into an uneasy doze he had come up with a plan of action, one he wanted to run through in his mind before he shared it with Sofia.

But first he'd make sure Sofia was actually still here.

He rose, dressed quickly and gave only a cursory look out of the curved window at the early morning sunshine, the leaves and branches of the trees completely still under the haze of heat from the cloudless blue sky. He headed out of his room and stood outside Sofia's, anxiety heightened as he knocked, replaced by both relief and a flutter of anticipation when he heard her voice. 'Marco?'

'It's me.'

'Come in.'

He pushed the door open and saw her sitting at the desk by the window, a closed sketchbook in front of her. In the light of day he could see that her room was at least in a better state than his. The walls were also in need of paint but the king-sized four-poster bed with its gold-leafed bed coverings looked comfortable. The mahogany desk came with an office chair and in truth the view from her window made up for everything—the smooth azure sea, the scrub of Mediterranean shrubs—and the scent of bougainvillea and lemon that wafted in from the courtyard.

'Good morning.'

'Good morning. Did you sleep okay?'

She moved her hand in a so-so gesture and he could see tiredness on her face, hoped his plan would help dissipate it. 'I've had an idea I'd like to discuss over breakfast. Which I am about to go and get now. Is there anything in particular you'd like?'

'Whatever you choose will be fine. I'll set the table.'

'I won't be long.'

True to his word Marco made sure his shopping trip was as quick as possible, didn't linger at the bakery, with its display of pastries, or the market, and although the next items on his list were a little bit harder to find he was back at the villa within an hour. Once again, the relief palpable when he entered the kitchen to find Sofia standing at the marble-topped counter, carefully arranging flowers in a vase.

'I hope it's okay to have picked these?'

'Of course.'

'I thought we could sit in the courtyard. There is a table and some chairs out there.'

'Sounds good. I got freshly baked bread, butter, jam and *torta Caprese* as well,' he said, naming the speciality chocolate cake made with almond flour. 'And coffee.'

'That sounds lovely,' she said.

He moved to the counter to unpack the bags and he was, oh, so aware of her, of a light floral scent, the brush of her arm against his causing desire to ripple in his gut. A desire he knew he had to quell.

Sofia was in his care, she needed protection and he had no intention of making her feel he expected anything in return, the idea repugnant. Seven years ago, he'd been worried about spooking her with a kiss. That had not changed. Kissing her would be wrong; she was a sheltered princess destined for a political marriage. But the knowledge did nothing to lessen the tug, the allure, the way her vanilla scent dizzied his head.

Soon they were sitting outside at a small wooden table set on a mosaic-tiled area shaded by a canvas canopy and surrounded by thriving luscious bougainvillea and roses. 'You said you had an idea?' She buttered a piece of bread and spread it generously with jam.

He nodded. 'I've been thinking about what you told me and it does change things.'

She put her coffee cup down, her gaze direct. 'I understand. If you no longer feel you can help, I get it.'

'No.' He shook his head. 'That's not what I meant. At all. I want to help. But I think our original plan, the hide-out idea, won't work. Your father has too many resources. If he knows about the cleaning job and suspects you are in Naples, he will leave someone there. He may even leave someone on Capri.'

'But he won't find me here, in the villa.'

'Maybe not, but how long are you willing to hide out in this villa? And how will you achieve anything hiding out?'

Sofia bit her lip. 'But what else can I do?'

'I think you need to hide in plain sight.'

She frowned. 'I don't get it.'

'No one looking for you knows anything about me. They are looking for a woman on her own, a woman with no money, hiding out somewhere. A woman with long dark hair. So let's change it up. We cut your hair, maybe dye it and then you stay here with me, openly. If anyone shows any interest, we say you're an interior decorator and we're staying here for a few days for you to look at the house. Then instead of hiding out in the villa, unable to leave, you can be free. Free to look round Capri, walk where you want to walk, go where you want to go. Without asking anyone. Have some fun. If you're with me and you look different, even if there is a guard looking for you, they won't spot you. And I'll be with you the whole time as camouflage.'

'But someone may recognise you and wonder who the woman with you is and then work out it is me.'

'I have never been recognised in Italy. I am based in America and London mostly, and my only real claim to celebrity fame was my connection with Cynthia and that was years ago now.'

'So, you've no interest in being in the public eye?' she asked.

'None. When I was with Cynthia, I loathed the attention. People thinking they could ask anything they wanted.' His refusal to do a cutesy couple interview, his refusal in fact to do any interview, had been a bone of contention with Cynthia. But Marco had had no intention of discussing his childhood or his view on relationships and certainly didn't want any enterprising reporter finding out anything about Leo. 'I really don't think there is any risk. There is probably more risk of them finding you if we are hiding out. Someone will spot you through a window, wonder why you never go out, wonder why I am buying provisions for two people. I truly think my plan works. And it is definitely more fun.'

'But what about you? Surely you have better things to do than babysit me?'

'Actually, no, I don't.' The words were the truth. 'I'd taken some time off to sort the villa out anyway. Yesterday we talked about fun and I realised that I can't remember the last time I had any. This seems like an ideal opportunity for both of us. I would like to go around Capri with you, relax, have a real break. After a few days maybe everything will become clearer—you may hear from Rosa or something may happen on Palosia. We can reassess then, maybe you can go back to Naples. I want to do this.'

He held his breath, wanting her to agree. Her story last night, the wistfulness and urgency in her voice when she exhorted him not to take the everyday freedom to do as he wished for granted, had caught at him. Now he wanted Sofia to at least have a taste of those freedoms.

She smiled, a smile that lit up her whole face and seemed to light something inside him too. 'Then so do I.' She touched her hair. 'I did think about trying to look different, but I didn't want to risk a hairdresser so I bought some dye. I even did the allergy test. But then I was too chicken to do it. I mean, my hair is so dark, what if it goes orange or something and I look even more noticeable?'

'I'll do it,' he said. 'Cut it and dye it. Tell me what dye you tested.'

She looked at him doubtfully. 'Have you ever cut hair before?'

'No, but I'm pretty sure I can do it.' After all, once he had sculpted clay, smelted copper. For an instant he recalled the feel of the clay beneath his fingers, the sheer joy of spinning it, moulding it, creating something with his own hands, the intensity, the feeling of fusion.

And whilst he didn't believe he could ever recapture that sense of creativity, he did believe he could do this. He looked at Sofia, his mind working out the angles, the best way to frame the beauty of her face, and he was struck anew by that very beauty.

The high slant of the cheekbones, the wide

eyes, the blue so dark and so clear, the long lashes, the sweep of her nose and the cast to her jaw that combined strength with delicacy. His gaze lingered on her lips, lips that he'd kissed, tasted, revelled in. Lips that he wanted to kiss again, even though he knew he wouldn't, couldn't. Not now he knew where she was from, the mores and rules and etiquette of her life. Not now when he understood the extent of the trust she'd put in him by revealing who she was.

So he wrenched his gaze away, and tipped his hands up. 'If you're willing to let me try.'

'I'm sure you can do a better job than me. So yes, please.'

'There's no time like the present. I'll pop back out and get the dye. I bought everything else when I was out earlier.'

An hour later they were standing in her en suite bathroom, facing the gilt-framed mirror set into the marble-tiled walls.

'I'm thinking a bob down to just above your collarbone?' he suggested and when she nodded, he continued. 'I'll wash it first, if that's okay? I think it will make it easier for me, start the creative process.'

'I'm in favour of anything that does that.'

Once he'd rigged up the hand shower over the curve of the gleaming white double sinks, she sat with her head tipped back over the sink and he started to lather in the shampoo, aware of tension in her body. Not surprising given the amount of stress she was under.

Slowly he started to move his fingers in firm gentle circles and she exhaled and he felt the tension gradually seep away, only to be replaced by tension of a different kind.

The room was, oh, so quiet, just the sounds of the birds from outside, a gentle breeze wafting in carrying the scent of flowers, of verdant greenery.

And now the silken feel of her hair under his fingers, her sheer proximity were making the breath catch in his throat. She'd closed her eyes, and he could see the length of her dark lashes, the flawless creamy skin. As he continued the massage with circular rhythmic strokes she made a small noise; a catch between a moan and a sigh, and he knew she was picking up the sheer sensual pleasure, aware of the current that was now impossible to ignore. A faint flush crept over the high cheekbones and her eyes flew open, eyes that held shock and desire. Her lips parted and all he wanted was to kiss her.

But he couldn't, wouldn't.

Instead, he stepped back, even as desire twisted his gut, urged him to throw caution to

NINA MILNE   121

the wind, told him there was no harm in one
kiss. But there was. One kiss would never be
enough, he knew that, the idea shocking—how
could Sofia arouse such strength of feeling in
him, something that felt like more than simple
physical desire, something that drove him to almost want something he knew couldn't work?
All the more reason to remind himself Sofia
was off limits. 'Time to start the cut,' he said,
aware his voice sounded over-hearty.

Somehow as he cut it was easy to work out
exactly what to do, the best way to frame her
beauty, to accentuate the impact of her eyes, to
showcase the classic structure of her face and
the wide, beautiful smile.

'Right. You can open your eyes now.' Eyes
she had kept resolutely shut. 'What do you
think?'

He'd cut a lot, her hair now a sleek crop of
glossy dark hair, cut close to her head, the ends
reaching the curve of her jaw line, her graceful neck now exposed, and his fingers tingled
with a desire to brush the nape.

'I've cut it so you can have a central parting and slick it down or you can get rid of the
parting and push it back.'

As he spoke, he demonstrated both styles,
tried to keep his breathing even as he felt her
shiver when he did inadvertently brush the

nape of her neck. A shiver that seemed to reverberate back to him.

'What do you think?' he asked.

'I… I love it.' Her voice held a certain wonder as she stared at her reflection, one hand going up to smooth her hair. 'I look so different.'

'Wait until I've done the dye.'

And two hours later they both surveyed her reflection and her eyes widened. The dye wasn't dramatic but her hair was a tone lighter, a deep brown highlighted with strands of copper that glinted in the late morning sun. Rising, she turned to face him. 'That's incredible. I don't just look different. I feel different. Like a different person. I think it will work. I really don't think a guard would recognise me.'

'Then your days of freedom start now. What would you like to do?'

'First? I need some new clothes, something to change my image. These…' She gestured to the long baggy navy skirt and long-sleeved dark blouse. 'These don't really make me blend in. I'd love to wander round the shops, maybe stop somewhere for coffee.'

'Free to do whatever you want, whenever you want.' He quoted her words from the night before.

'Exactly.'
'Then let's go.'

As they stepped out into the warmth of the late morning sunshine, Sofia tried to wrap her head round the concept of this sudden, unexpected freedom. As they walked along the pathway leading to the villa, past the grey stone walls and onto the pavement, she felt impervious to danger, able to revel in and appreciate the warmth of the rays, to inhale the hazy scents of sun and lemon, to look around and take in the brightness and vivacity of the flowers, the gloss and whitewash of the buildings.

But now more than anything she had an awareness of Marco, his proximity, his woodsy scent, the way the sunlight glinted on his blond hair... Everything about him causing ripples of desire to cascade over her skin. Her whole body still on high alert from when he'd massaged her scalp, the feel of his fingers, the strength, the tactility, the sensations he'd aroused still bubbling and seething inside her.

Made even more exhilarating by how different she looked, how different she felt, as though her skin were glowing, not from the Capri sun, but the sheer heat Marco generated, the memory of his fingers brushing the nape of her neck. Her whole body full of unfamiliar sensations, a yearning, a need, a heat.

Then they reached the winding narrow streets of Capri's centre and she truly was just one of the many, generating no interest, with no chaperone, no schedule, no timetable in a public place. And it was glorious to be able to walk with anonymity and security, taking in the beauty of her surroundings.

The stylish historic buildings, the abundance of cacti, aloe vera and exotic plants she couldn't name interspersed throughout, in alleyways and also atop the flat rooftops that characterised so many of the houses.

Then they arrived at the shops themselves, a street lined with designer shops, luxurious, exclusive brands displayed in glittering, artistically designed window fronts.

'This street has been around for a long time,' Marco said. 'Two thousand years ago it was where the cisterns were located. You can still see the bricks in the arches along the street. So once this was where rainwater was collected and stored, water that was vital for the island.'

'And now it's somewhere where the rich congregate to buy less than essential items. But I suppose you can argue it's what Capri is famous for so it is still essential. For its economy.' She glanced in one of the windows. 'But definitely out of my price range. Isn't there another famous shopping street with more local stores?'

Marco nodded. 'I know which one you mean. Once it used to be where all the local shops were, so the butcher, fishmonger and so on. Some of them are still there, but there are a lot of others now too, including some clothes boutiques.'

'Perfect.'

They made their way through narrow arch-covered alleys, vaulted houses, and soon enough Sofia gestured to a shop that at least looked relatively affordable.

'I'll try here.'

She stepped inside, felt a flicker of anxiety as the shop assistant greeted her. But the elegant woman gave no hint of recognition, simply offered help if needed. Relieved, Sofia picked two dresses that caught her eye and headed to the changing rooms.

Minutes later she surveyed her reflection, the clothes the finishing touch in her transformation. The dress was something she would never have been able to wear in Palosia, and she loved it. It was short by royal Palosian standards, the silk folds falling to just below the knee. The pattern reminded her of exotic plumage, orange, blues and reds, a pattern of flowers, trees and birds that was elegant rather than garish. The whole cinched with an orange sash-like belt.

She could just about afford this, another dress and a few other essentials. And she would still be left with enough if she eked it out so that she wouldn't have to ask Marco for anything over the next few days. But then what? She pushed the question away, didn't want to let the exhilarating sense of freedom dissipate, took one last glance in the mirror, and anticipation swirled inside her. What would Marco think of her new look?

After paying for her purchases, she exited the shop and a sudden shyness struck her, caused her steps to falter slightly. Then Marco turned, took in her appearance and shyness morphed into a sheer thrill of satisfaction at the look of appreciation in his eye. She heard the rasp in his voice. 'You look beautiful. Radiant.'

'Thank you.' She grinned at him and did a little twirl, revelled in the swirl of the silk around her legs, the sun on her bare shoulders. 'It feels so very different.'

'Shall we head to the square for lunch?'

'That sounds perfect.'

As they walked, he glanced at her. 'Different how?' he asked. 'What sort of clothing is traditional on Palosia?'

'Nowadays most people have relaxed the traditional approach and women wear a mix of the more traditional kaftans and more modern garments, jeans, T-shirts, sun dresses. But not Rosa and myself. My father insists on us "embracing tradition" to ensure we "keep the dignity of royalty and do not draw disrespectful attention".' The truth of it was that King Fiero didn't want his daughters to draw *any* attention, he would prefer them not to exist at all, their existence a reminder of the sons he didn't have. And Sofia a reminder of his own humiliation.

But now all such thoughts fled as they approached the *piazetta* and she blinked, felt as if she were entering a different world where time had stood still. The medieval church and picturesque bell tower, the scattered tables fronting a number of cafés served by waiters clad in cream jackets. She followed Marco to a free table and sat gazing round at the throng of people, inhaled the tantalising aromas of coffee, the pervading scent of lemons mixed with a baking scent redolent of sugar and spice.

She scanned the menu and smiled up at the waiter who appeared almost instantly.

'I'd like a Caprese salad, please.'

'Make that two,' Marco said and the waiter nodded and glided away.

'It's so…picturesque,' she said and she couldn't resist, delved into her bag and pulled out the sketchbook she carried everywhere.

'Do you mind if I make some sketches?'

'Go ahead.'

She opened the book to a fresh page and started to outline the scene, glanced up to explain.

'It's for ideas. If I draw the architecture, capture the lines, it sparks ideas for interior-design themes.' She sighed. 'I know there is a chance I'll never get to use any of them, but I enjoy sketching and it makes me feel like I am doing something positive about becoming an interior designer. Even if I know it's a dream that probably won't materialise.'

'Tell me about the dream,' he said. 'Do you have a specific goal?'

She nodded. It wasn't something she'd share with anyone but, here and now, sitting anonymously amongst the crowd of people, for a few hours she was going to allow herself to believe in a life where anything was possible. 'I'd love to work on fabulous places like palaces and villas, but also on different types of housing. On Palosia there is a housing shortage. People are still living in buildings that should have been condemned years ago. I'd like to knock them all down and start again, but I'd like the houses to be designed in an affordable, functional but also beautiful way. Beauty doesn't have to be expensive; it can be simple and comfortable without being stark or minimalist. I'd love to get involved with that. I'd like to design nurseries where women could have childcare so they could work. And I'd love to renovate historic buildings as well.'

He gestured to the sketchbook. 'Can I see?'

Sofia hesitated, unsure about showing something so important to her to anyone, beset by fear that a negative judgement would destroy her enjoyment. But the hesitation was only momentary; if she was serious about interior design she could hardly refuse to show people her ideas. 'Sure, but bear in my mind these are just ideas,' she settled for as she handed the book over, tried to keep her tone breezy, to stay relaxed as he turned the pages, tried to look as though her nerves weren't on the rack.

Relief arrived in the form of the waiter bearing their salads and she looked down at the vivid red of the tomatoes, the bright white of the mozzarella drizzled with oil and sprinkled with basil that smelt utterly divine. Tasted a forkful and let out a sigh of appreciation. 'This is delicious. I have no idea how something so simple can taste so good. It must be the freshness and quality of the produce. And this oil is definitely top-notch quality.'

Marco tasted his and nodded. 'This is pretty good,' he agreed, but his voice sounded absent-minded and he returned his attention to the sketchbook. 'And these are really good,' he said after a few moments. 'Really, really good.' Sofia released the breath she hadn't realised she was holding as she heard the sincerity in his voice. He pointed to the page he was looking at. 'That's the villa.'

She glanced at the page where she had sketched an idea for the large reception area of the villa. The wide arched window looking out at the garden showed the current patio adorned with a swinging basket chair, potted shrubs and plants and a sprawl of benches. The room itself with a striking rug, curved, elegant yet comfortable sofas and an arrangement of circular glass-topped tables. Arched art deco doors that complemented the architecture along with a dramatic hanging chandelier-type light.

'This is brilliant.'

'I couldn't sleep last night so I was just playing around with ideas.'

'I didn't know interior designers hand-sketched,' he said.

'Not all of them do. I can do computer drawings and plans as well. But, for me, there is something real, something authentic about hand-drawing. So here, if I sketch this square rather than take a photo or look it up on the Internet, I feel I am capturing its essence from my point of view and I can use that concept, which is unique.'

Marco pushed his empty plate aside and flicked through the sketchbook again. 'Would you consider drawing more sketches? I don't want to take away from having fun, but I'd love to have your ideas for the whole villa. If you stay long enough, I'd be willing to give you the project, providing the rest of your ideas are as good.'

Sofia stared at him. 'You don't have to do that. You can afford the best interior designer in the country.'

'I know I could. But I like these. I like your approach and I like your vision. If you don't feel able to commit to seeing through the whole project, I could still use your ideas as a blue-print.'

Sofia wondered if she should pinch himself, tried to think straight. 'You're sure this isn't charity?' Maybe he was humouring her, would accept the sketches but never ever use them.

'I'm sure. I wouldn't lie to you.' The words were deep and she sensed how important his integrity was. 'So will you do it?'

'Yes. I would absolutely love to. To actually design something and know my ideas will be converted into something real… That's beyond anything.' Happiness bubbled up inside her.

'We'll work out a fee.'

'Absolutely not. After all you have done for me, I will not accept payment.'

'Then it's no deal,' he said. 'I offered you a sanctuary because I wanted to. I'm offering you a job because it benefits me and I will pay a fair price for it.'

'I…' She grinned at him. 'Then thank you.' And whether he liked it or not she would pay him rent for the use of the villa out of the money he paid her. Money she would have earnt doing something she loved. Her smile widened. 'I'd like to start as soon as possible.' She looked round the crowded square. 'Could we go somewhere quieter so I can ask you some questions?'

'Sure. I know the perfect place.'

CHAPTER NINE

MARCO WAS AWARE of a sense of anticipation as they approached the port, a buzz of hope that Sofia would like his plan for the next few hours.

She glanced around at the crowds, a small endearing frown on her face. 'Where are we going?' she asked.

'I thought we could take a boat trip round the island. I've chartered a private yacht so we can talk in peace and not be noticed.'

Her smile was all he could have hoped for, her face lit up as she emitted a small chuckle. 'I was thinking of a tucked-away corner in a garden somewhere, but this sounds way more...'

'Fun?' he asked and she nodded, before her expression clouded slightly.

'It's okay. The captain only knows me as Marco and he didn't bat an eyelid. I told him it was a business meeting so we'd appreciate privacy rather than a guided tour and he's good with that. He's probably used to it; Capri is full of people richer and more famous than I am.

'It's even easier to fly under the radar here. I guess that never really happens for you.'

She shrugged. 'Yes and no. Because my father insists on us having a very sheltered life there isn't anything very much for a reporter to ask about. But when we do carry out any public duty we are scrutinised in detail and if we generated even a whisper of scandal it would be frowned upon.'

Which must have made Eli's betrayal all the worse to bear and made her all the braver for refusing to marry Eduardo. Admiration touched him anew, along with a renewed determination to make sure she enjoyed the time she had to be free from scrutiny. Before she had to return. The idea of her leaving struck a sudden discordant note, a memory of seven years ago when she'd gone, leaving him…bereft.

He shook the thought away. That had been different. Back then he'd believed her to be in danger, hadn't known who she was or where she'd gone. He'd been worried, frantic. This time he knew the facts, understood the parameters.

And the most important thing now was fun.

'So let's get on board,' he said.

Fifteen minutes later they were sitting at the

front of the fifty-foot yacht, cold glasses of champagne in hand as the boat glided over the water. Marco knew he should perhaps be looking at the scenery, after all it was incredibly beautiful, the sweeping heights of the limestone cliffs, the glimpses of hidden coves and caverns and the loom and jut of the overhead rock formations that protruded from the azure blue of the salt-tanged sea. But instead, he couldn't take his gaze from Sofia, saw the sparkle in her eyes and recalled her vivacity, the gesture of her hands as she'd spoken of her love of her work.

Work that intrigued him; he wondered if she fully appreciated the raw talent she had. The ability not just to capture proportion and detail but also to give her sketches life so they jumped off the page.

Her enthusiasm had reminded him of how he had once felt about his art, his creations, his dreams. Now, watching her, he wanted to etch her face onto his brain, because, one way or another, she would go back to Palosia and would be lost to him. And again, the reminder brought on a sense of loss. Not for himself, he told himself, it was the idea that her talent wouldn't be given its scope, that perhaps she too would lose the joy in her own creativity as he himself had.

She looked at him. 'What are you thinking?'

'How a princess can be so beautiful and so talented,' he answered truthfully, and was rewarded with a shy smile.

'With the help of a billionaire with a hidden talent for cutting hair.'

'That doesn't explain the talent.'

She tipped her head to one side. 'I'm not sure if it is a talent,' she said. 'Sketching buildings and interiors is something I've always done, something that I could do that was mine and no one could take away from me.' She sipped her champagne. 'You inspired me,' she said.

'What do you mean?'

'When I came to Naples all those years ago, I'd stopped sketching; there didn't seem any point. It wasn't bringing me happiness any more—I looked at the piles of sketchbooks and it all seemed like a monumental waste of my time. Sketches no one would ever see, that I would never be able to use. Then I met you and I saw your work ethic, your belief in yourself, how much you cared about art and sculpture and what you did. It made me believe that my dream was still worth dreaming. When I got back, it wasn't easy. My father was livid I'd run away; life became full of even more restrictions, but I started drawing again. Because I remembered your passion and belief.'

'I'm glad that I helped in some way.'

She hesitated. 'What happened? I know you said you changed, you stopped being that person, but it's so hard to believe.'

Marco looked back across the chasm of time, to a time before Leo, a time when the world had seemed a different place with different priorities. A time when he'd been naïve and idealistic. 'I grew up. My priorities changed. I changed. Needed to succeed faster, differently.' Because he'd known he couldn't succeed creatively, because his ability to be an artist had vanished, under the bitter weight of betrayal, the desolation of grief.

But he wouldn't share that with Sofia. It was over, done with, he'd moved on. Hadn't he? Yet today, seeing her excitement stirred memories of the soaring exhilaration, the sense of commitment that bordered on obsession whilst working on something. How time vanished, how deep frustration and light happiness could coexist.

Enough. That was gone. That had been a different Marco. 'Now I get fulfillment from my company, watching it grow, seeing it succeed.' And that was true; he did get a kick, a buzz from his business. His idea.

'I'm glad,' she said, but he could hear the soupçon of doubt in her voice. 'But could you still sculpt as a hobby?' she ventured. 'I know you no longer want or need to make it into a career, but don't you miss it?'

'No.' The word came out harder than he'd meant it to and he pulled up a smile. 'I've moved on,' he said. 'You just happened to meet me in my idealistic dreamer phase.' To his relief the yacht approached the majestic iconic beauty of the Faraglioni rocks, which effectively brought the conversation to a close as they both gazed in awe at the three colossal formations that towered from the sea.

'They are incredible,' Sofia said softly.

He nodded, struck by the sheer beauty that seemed to enchant each stack, carved by nature millennia ago, sun hazed by the Mediterranean air.

'Legend has it that they were formed by Odysseus in ancient times. He was sailing through these waters and he was set upon by sea monsters. He escaped by throwing massive rocks into the sea and those rocks were the start of the Faraglioni we see today. Other myths say that mermaids lived around the rocks and used to lure unsuspecting sailors off course. The one I prefer though is the idea that the rock would glow luminescent in the dark and act as lighthouses to help sailors in distress.'

'Those stories make them seem even more

magical,' she said. 'I can almost see the mermaids swimming through the arch, clinging to
the side of the sailors' boats, trying to entice
them. Maybe it wasn't their fault, maybe they
didn't know what they were doing, thought
they were leading them to a life of happiness. And I can see them glowing like bea-
cons of nature offering a light towards a path
of safety.' She looked at him. 'Because nothing is black or white in this world, is it? There
is good and bad, temptation and safety in everything. Maybe that's why these formations
feel so powerful, so significant.'

For a fanciful moment he could imagine her
as a mermaid, a woman sent to tempt him.
Shaking the notion away, he took one last look
at the looming mystical shapes as the yacht
resumed its course over the shimmering blue
water.

Sofia smiled at him. 'Thank you for this.
Seeing those, seeing all of this—' she swept a
hand around to encompass the scenery '—it's
beautiful and it is inspiring too. It's made me
think of lots of themes and ideas for the villa.'
She delved into her bag and pulled out her note-
book. 'I can't believe I get to sit here doing this
and you are proposing to pay me for it.' Her
soft laugh pulled an answering smile from him.
'Do you mind if we get started?'

'Of course not. Go ahead.'

'You've bought the villa as a holiday home for your mum; ideally I'd meet with her but, seeing as that's not possible, can you tell me what she's like in terms of her taste? An overall idea to start with. There's no point me choosing an ornate chandelier or pursuing ideas of art deco if she is more of a minimalist. I am happy to do different ideas so she has a choice, but I'd like them to be ideas she would definitely consider.'

She looked at him expectantly and Marco opened his mouth and closed it again, realised he had no idea what to answer.

Seeing him struggle, Sofia said, 'Or I can try to be more specific. Does your mum prefer white walls or bright colours? Is her house cluttered or is she really organised? Does she like traditional or contemporary? What did you grow up with?'

'It's not that easy,' he said. When he'd been a child neither of his parents had given a damn about the interior of the house and their stance would always be to simply find fault with the other person's taste. 'My parents divorced when I was twenty-one and now this villa is for my mum and her new husband and family.'

She paused. 'I'm sorry about the divorce but

you must be happy that your mum has found happiness.'

'Yes.' Marco could hear the flatness in his voice. 'I am, of course I am. Happy for her. She's married a nice man and she has three stepchildren who are lovely and have welcomed her in. But... I don't really know them very well.'

'So, she married recently.'

'Five years ago.' Marco realised he'd folded his arms somewhat defensively and quickly unfolded them. 'It was when Krafty was beginning to take off and work has taken a lot of my time ever since.'

'It's okay,' she said softly. 'You don't have to explain. It's natural sometimes to feel a bit strange if your parent remarries.'

He shook his head. 'I don't feel strange. I'm truly happy for her and I don't bear any resentment at all. I just wanted her to have time to settle in with her new family.' As soon as the divorce went through, he'd worked out the best thing to do was slip into the background of his parents' lives. 'It was perfect that Lorenzo came with a ready-made family. And I'm glad they feel like real family to her.'

'Have you got siblings?' she asked.

He shook his head. 'That why I am so pleased for her that she is so close to Lorenzo's children.' Again there was that defensive note in his voice and he frowned. The last thing he wanted was for Sofia to believe he was jealous. 'You see, my mum always wanted a big family. But she couldn't because fairly soon after I was born my parents realised that they should never have got married in the first place. They fell out of love and it wasn't pretty. But they both loved me and they decided the best thing for me was for them to stay together, to stick it out, however unhappy they were.' He could hear the incomprehension in his voice. 'They were individually wonderful parents who stayed together for me. They spent years living their lives for me, now they deserve their own space and time. Without me.' And he meant that, wanted his parents to live their lives.

'They stayed together because they both loved you,' she said softly. 'There's a difference.'

'No.' He shook his head. He knew Sofia was trying to make him feel better but he refused to hide behind that argument. 'There isn't. They endured twenty years of misery, wasted their youth. My mum lost her chance to have a whole brood of children. For me. It doesn't make any difference if it was done through love or if I wish they hadn't.'

'But it was their choice and it wasn't your fault.'

'It wasn't my fault, but if I hadn't existed, they could have split up, gone and lived their own lives. The least I can do now is try to make up for that.'

'By staying out of their lives?' she asked.

'If need be, yes. They deserve that, a chance to live those lives. My mum has remarried, she has a new life.'

'The life she may have had if she hadn't had you?' she asked and there was an underlay to her tone. 'And your dad?' she asked.

'He moved back to Scotland. That's where he was born and grew up and I think he always missed it. He's happy too; he's bought a ramshackle old place in the Highlands and he is doing it up.'

'I'm guessing you haven't visited?' she asked.

'Not yet.' He tried to explain. 'They are both finally happy. When I go round to see my mum it is all so different—everyone is relaxed and smiling, you can see Lorenzo's love for her. There is no shouting and there are so many family jokes. Then when I see pictures of where my dad is, see how happy he looks in the quiet and the beauty and the peace; I wonder how he managed all those noisy years. I don't want to…rock the boat.' Didn't want to intrude upon an idyll with reminders of their awful marriage, or with reminders of Leo. After all, his parents had lost a grandson too. 'I want them to enjoy what they have now.'

'You make it sound as though they can't enjoy their new life if you are part of it,' she said. She moved closer to him and, reaching out, she brushed his cheek with her hand, the gesture so sweet and yet somehow so sensual he blinked. 'That's not true. I know it.'

'I'm sure you're right,' he said but he could hear the lack of conviction in his voice and they were both silent, looking out to the cerulean sea and precipitous shore, at the white and grey hordes of gulls that thronged the coastal rock, at the glint of sunlight on stone villas built into the cliffs.

Then she turned to him, a hint of resolution in her voice. 'I *am* right.' She hesitated and then continued. 'Because I know how it feels if a parent truly doesn't want you in their life.' She made a gesture. 'If you read up on Palosia you'll see what happened. My mum…she left when I was a baby, not even two years old. She did choose to leave an unhappy marriage. The marriage was doomed from the start; my mother was in love with someone else when my father met her. But he didn't care, he believes his royalty entitles him to whatever and whoever he wants and being thwarted simply made her more of a challenge for him. He claimed to fall in love and it was inconceivable to him that my mother, a mere commoner, wouldn't be honoured by his love and love him back. In the end she did capitulate, under pressure from her family, and maybe her head was turned by wealth and promises, the fact that her family would benefit. That's why I know it is better to have an arranged marriage between equals, where both parties gain something, so they can both be content with the terms.

'Because my mother wasn't content. How could she be? They weren't seen as equals. The court looked down on her as a commoner, though the people loved her. I believe she regretted her decision from the start, and so did my father. It must have galled him that his bride was clearly unhappy and once he had the prize, he found he no longer wanted it, rued the marriages he could have made. Marriages between equals. And she must have deeply regretted giving up the man she loved. Then I was born, a daughter instead of the son he wanted, another disappointment and he took it out on her. In the end I think she couldn't take it any more; one night she ran away, went back to her true love.'

'Leaving you?' Marco closed his eyes, imagined the baby Sofia waking one morning and her mother was gone, could only imagine the void that must have left.

'Yes. I have told myself again and again that she must have had her reasons. I try to put the best spin on it but…at the end of the day she left. I can understand her leaving but I can't imagine leaving my child behind. To not at least have tried to take me. Perhaps seeing me reminded her of my father, reminded her of the wrong decisions she'd made. Maybe she couldn't love me. Or maybe she made the decision not to waste her life, her youth. And taking me was too complicated, would have jeopardised her love.'

Her voice broke slightly and his heart went out to her. 'I'm sorry,' he said softly. 'Sorry she left. But it's not on you.'

'You can't know that,' she said softly. 'The facts show that she left me behind. If she'd loved me enough she would have taken me. Instead, she made a decision that her life without me away from her marriage was preferable to life with me in her miserable marriage. Your parents chose to stay in their marriage. They did it because they loved you enough that for them the misery they brought each other was worth the joy they got from parenting you. So don't feel guilty and don't think that their life is now better without you in it. I know you are doing it with the best intentions but I think you're all missing out. You are lucky to have two parents in your life who love you, who tried to put you first.'

Her words resonated and he wondered if she was right, wondered if perhaps his decision to give his parents space from him was misplaced. 'Thank you,' he said softly. 'I promise I will consider your words.' His heart twisted anew at what she had told him, the idea that she had grown up in the knowledge that her mother had abandoned her, the belief that there was something lacking in her. *If she'd loved me enough she would have taken me.*

The words seemed to still linger in the air and he reached out and took her hand in his. 'I do know my parents made their decision with my best interests at heart. Maybe your mother believed she was too.'

'I'd like to think that. That she thought it was too risky. I may have cried, screamed, alerted the palace guards. Or she may have been depressed, not thinking straight.'

'Or maybe she genuinely thought leaving you behind was the best thing for you. The same way my parents believed it was the best thing for me for them to stay together.' Just as he'd thought he'd done the best thing to let Leo go. He squeezed her hand gently. 'I truly believe that is possible.' He hoped she could hear the fervency in his voice, wanted to dispel the clouds of sadness in her eyes, shifted slightly closer in the hope his proximity would offer a sense of solidarity. 'Have you ever tried to contact her?' he asked.

'That's why I came to Naples,' she said. 'To try and track her down. This time and seven years ago. I don't know if she is in Naples, but that's where her family came from. I thought if I could find someone in her family, perhaps they could at least get a message to her. I didn't manage it the last time, but this time I have tracked down an address of someone I believe is a relative. I was on my way there when I bumped into you, but now it is too risky to go back to Naples. This time I have to hope that I find her before my father finds me.'

He considered her words and he saw how he could truly help her, on a practical level.

'If you give me the details, I can ask my solicitor to act as a go-between, try to initiate contact with your mother. In a way that keeps your initial involvement minimal, keeps you distanced and doesn't make it obvious that you are actually on Capri.'

Satisfaction touched him as her eyes lit up. 'Really? You'd do that?'

'Of course I would. It makes sense for you to keep a low profile and it will allow you to keep working on the villa.' To enjoy her time, her limited time. And it allowed her to stay with him, whispered a small voice in the back of his head, one that he shut down instantly. Reminded himself that Sofia was leaving, had a destiny to fulfil. One that did not include him.

Yet for an instant he wondered what it would be like if Sofia didn't leave. Remained here, on Capri or in Naples. What would he do? Would they spend more time together having more fun? More…

His brain shut down the train of thought. There could be no more of anything. Sofia wanted different things from life than he did. She wanted a family. And if she didn't have the prospect of an arranged marriage ahead of her, perhaps she *would* want the real thing. Love, the happy ending… The works. Marco didn't want any of that. So, whatever he and Sofia had here and now he wouldn't act on it. Couldn't. The thought of getting involved was too scary. The idea of building something in the knowledge that it might well go wrong, change, morph into something bitter and desolate, was too risky. His parents' marriage had gone from joy to misery, his time with Leila, with Leo, had gone from a place of trust and partnership and joy to misery. Leaving him alone, and now that solitude was his strength. His protection against further hurt or abandonment.

But that didn't mean he couldn't enjoy the here and now with Sofia; more than that, he could try to make this stay on Capri special for her, ensure she enjoyed her taste of freedom. So enough of all this analysis of impossible might-have-beens he didn't even want. It was time to have fun and he recalled her wishes of earlier, to enjoy simple everyday pleasures.

'I'll call my solicitor as soon as we dock.' He could see the ferry port approaching. 'And then would you like to head back to town and find a pizza place? I am pretty sure we can find a crowded, local place where no one will give us a second glance.'

'That sounds perfect.'

CHAPTER TEN

An hour later they *had* found the perfect place, were sitting on a restaurant terrace overlooking a panoramic view of the Capri shoreline. Sofia watched the rays of the setting sun shimmer and tiptoe across the water, the deep green fronds of leafy trees gently sway in the warm scented evening breeze and a sudden precarious happiness fluttered through her.

A happiness she suspected came not so much from the scenery, breathtaking though it was, but from the man sitting opposite her. A man she had confided in and who had confided in her. As she looked at him, he smiled. Her heart cartwheeled and, afraid her own answering smile was veering towards goofy, she hurried into speech.

'That is stunning and the vibe in here is perfect. Whoever designed it did a fabulous job.' She looked around at the tiled floor, the whitewashed walls, alleviated by arches painted a deep blue. 'The marble tables give a sense of both tradition and opulence and I love the lighting. It gives a touch of the industrial and then you have the traditional red and white checked cushions scattered round.'

'The menu is pretty good too,' he said as a member of the waiting staff arrived at the table.

'Is there anything you would recommend?' Sofia asked.

'*Signora.* To be truthful everything on the menu is beautiful. The chef uses only the best local produce to create a tomato sauce that is renowned through Italy. And here in the kitchens we have a pizza oven that is one of the oldest on the island.'

'Then I will keep it simple and have a margarita pizza, please,' she said.

'And I'll try the fried upside-down pizza with the speciality tomato sauce,' Marco said.

They ordered a glass of red wine each and the waiter left.

'There's something special about the idea you're eating a pizza that's so steeped in tradition. But in a place that is contemporary, with recipes that have a new twist to them. That's how I wish Palosia could be, a mix of the best of our traditions but with a contemporary twist.'

'How would you achieve it?'

She hesitated. 'Are you sure you want to know? You're not just being polite.'

'I am a hundred per cent sure. I know so little about your country and I'd love to know your ideas for it.'

The thought that he meant it, that he was actually interested in what she had to say, exhilarated her; the novelty almost fantastic. 'Well, for example, I'd love to promote the island for more than its olive oil. I know Capri has its own signature perfume; I wish Palosia would do the same. We have incredible flowers unique to the island and both Rosa and her mother are passionate, knowledgeable gardeners. I am sure they could work with a parfumier to create something wonderful.'

'Why don't they? That sounds like something that would be great for Palosia.' He leant forward and she could see his brain whirring. 'From an economic point of view as a business, but also it would increase the tourist trade, make Palosia better known and enhance the royal family's image.'

She sighed. 'My father wouldn't let them. Queens and princesses aren't allowed to work. He did allow Chiara, that's Rosa's mother, to set up a cooperative that helps Palosian women make traditional straw hats, but he only agreed to do that because it generated good publicity on the island at a time he needed it. But he definitely doesn't like what a success she has made of it.'

Marco looked puzzled. 'But your ideas would enrich the island. As its ruler he must want that. Have you ever talked to him about the ideas? Or could you talk to his advisors? Surely you of all people can persuade him— you're articulate, you're resourceful, you're bright, enthusiastic...'

Sofia couldn't help but smile—the compliments warmed her in an unfamiliar glow and her smile morphed to a low chuckle. 'Don't stop. Keep going. It's all music to my ears.' Without thinking she reached out, placed her hand over his, and bit back a small gasp, the touch electric. The past hours, the freedom, their proximity had fed the simmering attraction and now desire fizzed through her with a deep, unsettling heat. Her eyes roved his face, the strength and cragginess, the dark blond hair highlighted in the last dappled rays of the sun, and settled on his lips.

Then he smiled back, a long, decadent smile full of promise. 'I'm happy to comply. You're beautiful, you care about things, you're talented, you're kind, insightful...and right now all I want to do is kiss you.' He broke off and swore under his breath. 'Sorry. I shouldn't have said that.'

Maybe he shouldn't have but Sofia didn't care. The words had sent a thrill of sheer happiness, a satisfaction, straight through her along with an escalation of white-hot desire. All she could think about was how it would feel if he did kiss her. Because he actually wanted to, was consumed as much as she was. Now she was leaning forward and the only thing that saved her was the soft noise of their waiter clearing his throat.

Dammit. What was she doing? The whole point was to not draw attention to themselves, to look like colleagues. Colleagues would go out for pizza but they wouldn't end up in a lip lock.

The waiter discreetly deposited their wine in front of them and left and Sofia pulled a smile to her face, saw the rueful tilt tip his lips, saw too that desire still darkened his grey eyes. 'You don't need to be sorry,' she said. 'I…' Shyness tinged her cheeks. 'I'd like to kiss you too. But it's not a good idea.' Though suddenly she wondered why not.

'Not here and now. Or not ever?' he asked softly, echoing her thoughts.

She closed her eyes, opened them again. 'I don't know.' Honesty seemed to be the best policy. Part of her asked, could a kiss matter? The other part clanged a warning bell loud and clear. Attraction was a distraction and it wasn't something she could have, she knew that. Knew there were other things that were way more important. But those were things to think about whilst considering an arranged marriage. That wasn't on the table here. She shook her head; she'd said it herself—attraction was all about playing with fire. And fire was dangerous.

'It's okay.' Marco raised a hand. 'I'm sorry. I don't want to make things awkward. I really shouldn't have said any of that.' But now he smiled, a smile full of reassurance. 'Apart from when I said all the nice things,' he added. 'I meant every one. But now let's scrub all mention of kisses from the record and go back to our conversation. Deal?'

He lifted his glass and she smiled back at him. 'Deal.' She clinked her glass against his, unsure how easy it would be but determined to try.

He thought for a moment, clearly rethreading the conversational needle. 'So, to go back, have you tried talking to your father or his advisors about change?'

Sofia sighed. 'We don't really talk. If we have to have a conversation it is usually more of a shouting match but, in truth, he mostly pretends I don't exist. He certainly doesn't value my opinion enough to give my ideas any thought and his advisors take their cue from him.'

His forehead creased and she could tell he was going to try to come up with a strategy.

'Nothing will change that.'

'Are you sure? It's not like you to give up. Look at your interior-design aspirations.'

'This is different.' Hesitating, she sipped her wine then placed the glass back down. 'I'd like to explain, but I don't want to sound self-pitying. It is as it is and I know there are millions of people in the world who would think it's ridiculous for a princess to complain about anything.'

'You aren't complaining, or self-pitying,' he said. 'I'd like to understand.'

'Nothing will shift our father's stance on Rosa or me. He would never give us equality or freedoms. He resents us too deeply, both of us for being girls and he despises me because I am a reminder to him of his own folly in marrying my mother, a daily reminder of his own humiliation. That turned the disappointment he'd felt at my gender into something worse.' Her voice matter-of-fact. 'I brought him no joy at all to balance against the misery he associates with me.'

Shock and compassion showed in his eyes. 'But you are his daughter. His eldest child. That must count for something in terms of the succession.'

'Traditionally a woman cannot rule, but she can bear the male heir. But my father does not believe I am worthy, believes my blood is tainted. My whole life he has made it clear he doesn't consider me to be truly royal.' She kept her voice matter-of-fact, had absolutely no wish to invoke pity. 'When I was fourteen, I overheard a conversation saying that my father had cut me out of the succession. I didn't believe it.' Reliving it now, she heard her voice crack slightly. 'I went straight to confront him, challenge him. I can remember what he said, word for word.'

In that moment she was back in the royal stateroom, listening to King Fiero's harsh voice, heaping scorn and derision over her. '"You are the daughter of a commoner, a woman who had no principles or morals, your blood is tainted and I will not allow it to poison Palosia's royal bloodline. Your child will not so much as touch the throne. Rosa's son will be heir. You shall have no influence or say. Because to me you are nothing. I will support you because I have no choice and in return you will obey my bidding and in time you will marry who I tell you to marry. Remember your place or it will be far the worse for you. And your sister.'"

There was a silence and she saw Marco's hands slowly clench into fists, his mouth set in a grim line. 'I don't know what to say. I cannot imagine what that did to you.'

'For a while it crushed me. Not because I begrudge Rosa her position. I don't.' That was the truth. She had felt saddened that she was deemed unworthy of the position she had believed was hers by right, that she would have no part in her country's future, but mostly, 'It was the idea that I was unworthy to have any connection to my country, that I was tainted. Sometimes it does feel that way to me. There was a reason she abandoned me. Either my own shortcomings or hers.'

'No.' The word was torn from him.

She shrugged. 'I know I look like my mother, but I don't know anything else about her. To my father, to the whole court, she is persona non grata, vilified as an adulteress, a person with no concept of duty. It was after that conversation with my father, when I realised the truth depth of his loathing of her and me, that I knew I had to find her. See her for myself.

And now maybe I will. Thanks to your offer of help. I feel that if I can find her, meet her, talk to her, it will get me understanding and some form of closure. Then I can return to Palosia.'

Before she could say more the waiter arrived with their food and she sat back as he placed their plates in front of them and then in a deft movement tugged a handful of herbs from the plants growing in the terracotta pots that lined the terrace and sprinkled them over the food. The addition enhanced the already tantalising aroma wafting up from the plates.

She smiled up at him. 'Thank you. This looks incredible,' she said.

Marco nodded, added his thanks but he sounded almost absent-minded and she sensed his mind wasn't really on the food. An idea backed up when the waiter left and he didn't even glance downward, left his cutlery un-touched. 'Or you could tell your father you aren't going back,' he said. There was a pause and her heart did a funny little hop, skip and a jump. Stay here. With Marco. Walks through Naples together, going out for dinner without fear of being identified, without the fear of being caught and dragged back. More pizza, perhaps cooking a meal together. A job, a real job, completing Marco's villa, meetings with Marco, with his mother.

But then he gave his head a small shake as if dispelling his own thought process.

'Don't go back,' he repeated. 'Relocate. You could go anywhere in the world, build yourself a life abroad. As an exiled princess.'

Sofia blinked, realised the absurdity of her own thoughts. Of course he wasn't suggesting she stay with him. The idea *was* absurd. Marco had his own life, had made it plain he wasn't on the market for *any* sort of relationship. More to the point, she didn't want to stay with him; what would be the point? There could be no future in it. She wanted a family, he didn't.

So his suggestion had nothing to do with them, because there was no them and never could be. He was simply suggesting she leave Palosia, relocate 'anywhere in the world'.

'I can't do that.'

'Why not? Your father has taken so much from you. You owe him nothing.'

'It's not about him. My father believes my blood is tainted, perhaps it is. But Palosia is my country and the thought of losing it, being exiled, isn't something I can allow to happen.' Images of the island came to her and she leant across the table. 'I wish you could see it. The olive groves, the lush beauty, the scent on the air from the trees and all the flowers. But it's more than that. If I leave then I am proving my father right. That I am like my mother, that I too have run away from my duty and responsibilities as a princess of Palosia.' And that was not a possibility, not a scenario she could ever accept or initiate.

'But what about your life?' he asked.

'That is my life. To be a princess. And it's more than that. I can't and I won't leave my sister.' Her own words triggered a sense of guilt that she had, however briefly, contemplated the idea. A further confirmation if she had needed it that attraction, the pull and tug of whatever it was she felt for Marco, was dangerous. Messed with her head and made her forget the things that were really important. Like Rosa. She must never risk any emotion that could cause her to make bad decisions, to prioritise love over family. As her mother had.

'If my father banishes me I may never see her again. And that is not happening. Rosa is—' She broke off, marshalled her thoughts, wanted him to understand. 'When Rosa was born, I was only three years old but the minute I saw her I felt this incredible urge to protect her. She looked so small, so vulnerable and I vowed I would always be there for her. And I still feel like that.'

'Of course you did.' Now his voice was deep

with understanding. 'You must have believed that perhaps her mother would leave as well.'

She nodded, touched at how he instantly got it. 'I must have, and even when it became clear Chiara wouldn't do that I…could never be sure of what would happen. My stepmother is a truly good woman, but it is my father who calls the shots. He could have banished Chiara because he needed a son and after Rosa there were no more pregnancies. That made him dislike Rosa almost as much as he loathes me. So, I have always tried to be there for her. Tried to stand between her and my father. Because Rosa isn't like me. She is one of the gentlest people I know. She always finds the good in people and she also has so much inner strength; she is beautiful inside and out. I can see why Chiara did stay.'

'So can I but don't ever believe that Chiara stayed because Rosa is better than you in any way.'

'I don't believe that. Or not exactly. But…'

'It must have been hard for you,' he said. 'That Rosa's mother stayed when yours didn't.'

'Sometimes it was. I did question what it was about me that made it okay to abandon me, but in the end I was glad that Chiara stayed. Was there for Rosa.'

'Then that makes you a good person, because

sometimes you must have had bitter thoughts but they didn't make you bitter. You didn't resent your sister, instead you were happy for her, cared for her, shielded her. That takes compassion and kindness and inner beauty.'

Sofia blinked back a tear at his words. 'But I was lucky as well. Chiara was not a wicked stepmother. She has always been kind to me and encouraged Rosa and me to be close. And I admire her for sticking out a marriage that diminishes her, where she is bullied and belittled.' She sighed. 'And over the years, as I've watched Chiara get frailer and weaker as a result, I do wonder if perhaps my mother was right to leave. But then I see the bond between Chiara and Rosa and I know Chiara never would.' A bond that sometimes made Sofia feel excluded, sad that she would never have that bond with a parent. Made her all the more determined to make sure she had that sort of bond with her own child, a bond she would never let anything break.

'I understand why you couldn't leave Palosia whilst Rosa was growing up. But Rosa is an adult now. You said yourself that she will soon be married, that it is her duty to have the royal heir. Surely then she won't need your protection any more, surely you are entitled to your own life now?'

'She still may need me. What if her marriage is miserable? I don't trust my father—we don't even know the identity of the man she is to marry. In any case, if I defy him he has it in his power to make sure I never see Rosa again. I can't and won't let that happen. I won't leave her to my father's whims.' As her mother had left her.

'I understand,' he said quietly. 'But I hope one day the situation changes. That you can to some degree follow your own dreams.'

'I will.' She could see a sadness in his grey eyes, a frustration that he couldn't come up with a solution. 'Truly, Marco, I have come to terms, made my peace, with my life. I will negotiate a good marriage, have a family and some freedom. I will be there for Rosa.' And she would prove to her father, to herself, that she was a true princess. 'I'm happy with it.' She smiled now, wanted to lighten the mood. Reached forward and touched his cheek gently. 'And right now I am happy to be here, to have this chance, be it a few days or a few weeks, to not be a princess, to experience this time. Here.' She held her breath and decided to speak truth. 'With you.'

The feel of his cheek under her hand, the rough six o' clock shadow, made her catch her breath as attraction shimmered and weaved in the air. And suddenly Sofia didn't care, wanted to give this attraction a bit more free rein. She was happy with the future fate and birth had destined her for but, in the meantime, her body, her heart, craved to experience this. At least a little bit.

And perhaps he felt the same, because now the sadness went from his face and he smiled; a smile that seemed to hold an infinite promise. 'Then let's make the most of it,' he said. 'I have an idea where we can go next.'

'Where?'

'It's a surprise,' he said.

CHAPTER ELEVEN

TWENTY MINUTES LATER they were standing outside an unassuming building, indistinguishable from any other trattoria, with its curved wooden door and low-key signage.

'Here we are,' Marco said as he pushed the door open. 'I know it would be easy to pass by but this is one of Capri's most visited nightclubs. I thought you may like the chance to experience some nightlife in a place where you can let your hair down if you want to or just watch and soak up the ambiance.'

'I'm not sure I know how to let my hair down,' she said quietly. 'As a princess one of the major rules is to always be dignified and calm. Though admittedly that isn't always my forte.'

'Apparently this is the sort of place where dancing on the tables isn't unknown. But its aim is to bring people from all walks of life together to simply enjoy themselves, listening to music in a place that combines history and the present day. That's why I thought it may appeal to you. It combines tradition and contemporary.'

She smiled, felt a happiness at the knowledge that Marco truly listened to her, heard her, saw her. Once inside, she looked around. The club was already crowded and there was a relaxed, inclusive vibe. The clientele was of all ages, shapes and sizes, dressed in styles ranging from jeans to party dresses and tuxedos. Exposed brickwork, rustic wooden tables scattered over the floor and a terracotta theme complemented by checked red and white tablecloths gave the interior the appearance of a typical trattoria. But there was a sense of anticipation, a buzz created by the posters and photographs that covered the walls, depicting the club's past and present. Pictures of locals and celebrities mingling illustrating the club's success in bringing people together.

Marco guided her to a seat and, a few minutes later, handed her a glass of champagne.

'To you,' he said.

She shook her head. 'To today,' she said softly. 'It has been a perfect day. So to today and…' She paused and as the singers started to tune up on the stage she felt a sudden, heady sense of exhilaration. What had she said earlier? That she wanted to enjoy this time as a non-princess. With Marco. 'To the night to come,' she said, told herself that she simply meant the time they would spend in the night-club, knew deep down that maybe she meant something more.

His grey eyes sparked, turned darker with a latent desire and she allowed her lips to curve upwards in a smile she *wanted* to hold allure. And as he clinked his glass against hers, he smiled back, a smile that held a promise, a depth, that made her shiver. 'To the night to come, may it be whatever you want it to be.'

Whatever she wanted it to be. The idea sent a thrill through her; she knew what she wanted it to be, she just didn't know if what she wanted was a good idea. Didn't know if it was brave or foolhardy to say what she wanted, do what she wanted. Because right now all she wanted to do was kiss him, to kiss him and be kissed back, to press her body against his and...

She blinked, forced herself to turn to the stage where the singers were warming up, hoped that music might somehow mitigate, push away, the feelings, the sensations, the yearning in her body.

'The main singer is the owner of the place,' he said and she could hear a hint of strain in his voice, see a tautness in his body as if he too was holding back with an effort. 'And the other members of the band are all family members. They play both traditional Neapolitan ballads and contemporary-style pop and everyone can sing along.'

To her own surprise Sofia found herself doing exactly that along with so many other people at neighbouring tables. All from the singer's ability to somehow draw them in, until everyone was clapping, laughing together with a palpable feeling of fellowship. The next song started and Marco rose to his feet, and she instinctively followed suit. Soon she was lost in the music, the rhythm and the beat of the tambourines, all the feelings and emotions of the day finding expression in the movement of her body.

Eventually she ceased, breathless and laughing, found herself leaning back against the warm, muscular strength of Marco's body as the singers sang a slower ballad that had everyone swaying. Now she closed her eyes, every sense heightened, every millimetre of her, oh, so aware of Marco and the press of their bodies together.

Until she knew that these feelings, this need, this yearning had to be assuaged. Whatever the cost, whatever the obstacles, she could not let this moment pass. And as the last lingering notes trembled through the air she turned, touched his cheek in a fleeting gesture. 'Is it okay if we leave now?' she asked, knowing they had to go before the last vestiges of common sense left her and she kissed him right here.

'Yes.' The one syllable echoed her urgency.

As they exited into the cool breeze of the still starlit sky, she realised it was the early hours of the morning. They walked in perfect synchronicity, propelled by the same sense of urgency until they reached a secluded spot, and she laid a hand on his arm. When he turned to face her, before she could change her mind, she stood on tiptoe and brushed her lips against his.

Heard his exhalation of relief as he pulled her closer into his embrace, his lips demanding more now and she felt a soaring sense of heady exhilaration, a knowledge that there was nothing more important than this, the shocking glorious pleasure his lips evoked. As if everything from the minute she'd set eyes on him in Naples had been leading to this crescendo of desire, this swirling, whirling, dizzying pleasure.

And she knew it couldn't be left at this, because this taste wasn't enough; her whole body was crying out for more.

She pulled back from the kiss, swayed and

he reached out to steady her, both their breathing ragged in the balmy air.

'We need to go back to the villa,' she said, didn't even recognise the voice as her own, and he nodded. Turning, they started the walk back, stopping occasionally to briefly brush lips until finally the villa came into sight. Then a few more steps and with a fumble of the keys they were inside and he was kissing her again with an added burning, mutual need. Until he pulled away, despite her small bereft gasp of protest.

'Sofia. I…you…'

She reached out, placed a finger on his lips, her whole being consumed. She heard the break in his voice, knew his need matched hers, understood what he was asking. Knew he needed to be sure this was what she wanted.

'I want this, Marco. I want you. If…if we don't do this, I know I will regret it for the rest of my life.'

It was all she needed to say. He stepped forward and in one fluid movement scooped her up into his arms, and she wrapped her arms round his neck as he carried her upstairs, pushed the bedroom door open with his foot and made his way over to the bed. Laid her down gently and she smiled up at him, her whole body trembling, aching with desire, filled with a need that only he could assuage.

Marco opened his eyes, aware of a deep languorous sense of contentment, shifted slightly to see Sofia, still asleep, her cheek pillowed on one hand, her other hand resting lightly on his chest. The sensation, both sweet and sensual, sent a warmth through his body, triggered memories of the previous hours. Hours filled with a bliss that transcended anything he had experienced before. The passion, the wonder, the intensity, laughter and joy as they had explored each other's bodies and ascended heights of fulfillment.

Yet through the contentment now stirred a sudden anxiety; Sofia had said she would regret not doing this for the rest of her life but suddenly Marco wondered if the opposite could be true. What if she regretted what she had done? After all, she was a Palosian princess, a woman who wasn't even supposed to spend time alone with a man.

The anxiety intensified. Seven years before he'd kissed her and whilst he knew now that hadn't driven her away, maybe it would have. If the guards hadn't found her, would she have left anyway? At some point or another, of course she would. The next day, week, month or year, the conclusion would be the same. Just as it would be now. But now he had done something he had vowed not to do. And he didn't know what the ramifications of that would be. If she regretted it maybe this time she would leave, and he would have driven her away.

As if she sensed his sudden unease, she opened her eyes, blinked and then smiled at him, a smile so sweet something tugged in his chest.

'Good morning,' she said. Then glanced at her watch. 'Or rather good afternoon.' She stretched languorously. 'That is the best night's sleep I've had…ever.' Now her smile widened impishly. 'It must have been all the activity.' The smile retreated slightly as she took in his expression.

'Marco? Is something wrong?' She moved her hand from his chest and shifted away, anxiety clouding the sparkle in her blue eyes. 'Did I do something wrong?'

'No.' Remorse shook him that she should even consider that, even as he understood why she asked. Her whole life she'd been told she was wrong, tainted, not good enough. 'No. Absolutely not. I was worried that *I* did something wrong.'

'You?' For an instant she looked puzzled and then she shook her head.

'You mean you think you shouldn't have, that we shouldn't have…that last night shouldn't have happened.'

'Something like that. You told me yourself that your culture, your traditions, mean you shouldn't even date a man, let alone…'

Sofia gave a sudden chuckle as he broke off. 'Let alone do any of the things we did.' She shifted back close to him again, leant up on one elbow. 'I promise you I do not regret last night at all. I do not believe in or agree with the rules and restrictions my father imposes on Rosa and myself. And if you're worried about the prospects of any arranged marriage, don't be. Most Palosians do not enforce rules as draconian as my father's are. Plus, any prospective husband will be more interested in my title, not any past relationships.' She raised a quick hand. 'Not that this is a relationship.'

Marco pushed away the idea of Sofia getting married. The idea of her being with anyone else sent denial, discomfort and irrational jealousy rushing through him. Which made no sense and he would not spoil 'this' with a dog-in-the-manger attitude. He reached up, twirled a strand of her glossy dark hair. 'So, what is this?' he asked.

'It's an…interlude,' she responded. 'I don't know how long I have here, with you, but I know and you know that it is time limited and I want to make the most of it. I want to enjoy it and look back with no regrets. Neither of us want or believe in love so this is perfect, an opportunity to create something precious, a brief moment in time, that has no impact on our futures.'

Her words made sense. They could enjoy something that could never get spoilt or sullied by the passage of time, or reality. There would be no time for attraction to fade, or incompatibilities to occur. There could be no betrayal of trust. They could simply enjoy their time together without worry or anxiety. And he vowed that he would do everything he could to make sure this interlude was everything Sofia wanted it to be.

'An interlude it is,' he said. 'What would you like to do first? We can go wherever you like.'

'Actually…' Sofia smiled at him '…how would you feel about remaining right here?' She shifted closer to him, her hand still on his chest.

'Hm, I think I could be persuaded. Especially if we…' He tugged her closer and whispered some particularly innovative ideas. 'I believe I know someone who once said attraction is overrated. Well, I'd like to challenge that assumption.'

She chuckled and said, 'Feel free to rise to the challenge.'

And then the chuckle developed into a sudden giggle at the infantility of the innuendo and he laughed too before tugging her into his arms.

CHAPTER TWELVE

AND THAT SET the scene for the next two days; they had picnic meals in bed, spent time sunbathing in the garden, where Sofia sat at the table, sketchbook in front of her, or borrowed his laptop to work. They discussed anything and everything under the sun, from films and books to the pros and cons of velvet cushions, from solar panels to wind energy, politics, and their favourite foods.

They took turns cooking for each other, fed each other olives, compared varieties of lemons and as each hour passed neither of them referred to anything in the real world and Sofia refused to acknowledge the ticking of the clock.

She opened her eyes one morning to find Marco standing by the bed holding a tray. 'Breakfast in bed,' he announced. 'I have warm fresh bread and cheese and strawberries and a chocolate sauce made with a few extra ingredients. A hint of chilli and a touch of vanilla. And I have some very good ideas involving the strawberries and chocolate.'

His words and the suggestive wiggle of his eyebrows made her laugh. But the laughter was accompanied by a shiver of anticipation that clenched her body with desire and she wondered anew how it was possible to feel like this. 'Perhaps we should start with the strawberries,' she suggested.

'Your wish is my command,' he said with a slow smile.

'Even better.' She reached for the jug of chocolate sauce. 'Let's get started.'

An hour later when they were finally eating the bread and cheese, sitting up in the bed, Sofia gave a contented sigh.

'I could get used to this,' she said. As soon as the words fell from her mouth, she regretted them, each word like a douse of cold water, and she struggled to retrieve them. 'You'll have to give me the recipe,' she added lightly, even as she tried to ignore the warning bell clanging in her head, wondered if this was how Pandora had felt when she opened the box. Because until now she would never have believed, never have dreamed, that attraction could lead to such soaring, glorious pleasure. Wouldn't have believed that a physical act could bring such gratification, in both the giving and receiving of joy. The sensations evoked by Marco's touch were beyond description, could reduce her to a trembling, shivering need and yearning. But what was even more heady, more dizzying, was the fact that it was reciprocal, that he felt a desire that matched her own. It seemed impossible that she, a princess of Palosia, could act with such utter shameless, greedy abandon.

But what was most alarming was the persistent feeling that this was about more than attraction. There were times when she would half wake in the night, aware of a sense of safety and security in his arms, her head on his chest, her arm wrapped over his chest, or her body spooned or cocooned against his.

She shook her head, told herself it was the novelty factor, combined with the forbidden-fruit aspect. In the end, this would wear off and leave nothing behind. The life she was destined for might not include this type of attraction but it would include things that were of way more importance. Somehow right now, though, that was hard to believe. The thought of leaving Marco for marriage to some other yet to be identified man made anxiety unfurl in her tummy. Made her want to turn and wrap her arms around Marco, cling to him and never let go. *Never?* What was the matter with her?

Now panic added to the anxiety, galvanised her to speak.

'I think we should leave the house, go and see something on Capri.' Perhaps the fresh air would clear her head, shift her priorities back into place. Perhaps seeing Capri, mingling with the crowds, would remind her this was and could only be an interlude.

'Good idea.' She heard the hint of constraint in his voice, wondered if her earlier words had made him think she'd been angling for more of a commitment. Another unwelcome thought and a stark reminder that Marco did not want a relationship. Full stop.

'Great. There are things I want to see before we have to get back to our normal lives,' she said with determined cheerfulness that rang false in her ears. Because right now she couldn't think of a single one, wanted to remain in the villa in a cocooned bubble where she could stop time, let the interlude play on some sort of time loop.

'Sure.'

Now she thought she detected a soupçon of relief and a pang of hurt prodded her. One she recognised as irrational; this was *her* idea. But what if Marco had been feeling claustrophobic? What if he had been humouring her the past days—trying to give the poor princess a good time before she returned home? *Enough*. That wasn't fair because that was the whole point. To have a good time before she went home. 'I'll be ready in half an hour.'

Once ready, Sofia glanced at her reflection, saw how different she looked, suspected it was more than the hairstyle change. There was something in her expression, her eyes, the way she stood; she *felt* different. Presumably it was a temporary thing. Down to some sort of hormonal reaction that would fade in the same way the hair dye would.

Turning from the mirror, she headed to the front door, where Marco stood. His blond hair was shower damp, and he looked so damn gorgeous her heart did a hop, skip and a jump and she had a sudden urge to run to him, wrap her arms around him, pull him straight back to bed. Forcing her steps to slow down, she exhorted herself to calm down. But for the first time in days, she felt a tug of fear that a palace guard would be waiting outside, that this interlude would be ended before she was ready. She would be ready, just not yet.

She told herself not to be foolish, there was no reason to believe a guard could have tracked her down. Even if one had and she had to return today, her sister, her true life, would be waiting. There was no future with Marco; she didn't *want* a future with Marco.

'You okay?'

His voice was deep, reassuring and caring and despite herself, despite everything she knew, she pictured a future with Marco. Waking up with him every day…an image of Marco holding a baby, their baby, a little girl with Marco's blond hair and her blue eyes. *Enough.* She was being ridiculous.

'I'm fine,' she said. 'Just thinking about where to go.'

Before he could respond his phone buzzed, he listened for a few minutes and after a short conversation he hung up, turned to her and she could see the excitement in his face. 'That was my solicitor. They have found your mother.'

Sofia froze, stared at him wide-eyed.

'She has agreed to meet you. *If* that's still what you want.'

'I… I don't know…what I want.' She felt shaky, the emotions of the past few minutes converging.

He put a steadying hand on her arm, and his touch felt so reassuring, so right. 'Then take your time to decide,' he said.

But there was no time. To have got this far and then be thwarted would be unbearable. 'I need to see her,' she said. 'Otherwise, I will always wonder.'

'Understood.' He took his phone out of his pocket and as he started the call, further ramifications loomed. Once she'd seen her mother she'd achieved her goal here. It would be time to go home. Leave here, leave Capri, leave Marco. She pushed the panic down; there was still the villa, still time whilst she figured out the situation on Palosia. Right now, she needed to think about the fact that she was going to see her mother. For real.

'Early evening,' he said after a five-minute conversation. 'We can meet at a solicitor's office in Capri.'

Sofia nodded. 'Thank you,' she said. 'For making this possible.' She glanced outside at the bright early morning sun; already she felt restless, a nervous energy pulsing inside her as she calculated the hours left until the meeting.

Marco studied her face. 'Let's go out. It'll make the time go quicker.'

'I'm not sure I want to risk it.' But then again what if the guards did track her to the villa? 'Plus I don't think I can focus on anything touristy. Or eating anything.'

'I get that. I thought we could find a secluded stretch of beach. We can walk and talk or just sit and look at the sea. Whatever works for you.'

'That sounds perfect.' And once again, it warmed her that he understood her without a need for explanation.

Half an hour later, having stocked up with drinks and snacks, they were back on a boat, a smaller one this time, gliding over the sparkling turquoise waters. And as she listened to the squall of the gulls, she tried to imagine seeing, actually *seeing*, her mother. Speaking to her. The woman she'd pictured so many times, had tried so desperately to remember, never sure if the images she had were real or a figment of her imagination. A slight woman with long dark hair, holding her, stroking her head and singing a lullaby to put her to sleep. Fact or wishful thinking? Perhaps now she'd find out.

She came out of her reverie as the boat bumped to shore.

'We're here,' Marco said and she scanned the unpopulated cove, saw that Marco had located one of the very few coves in Capri that boasted sand at all, saw the sun glint off the golden grains and the rockier inland, looked at the loom of the rugged precipitous cliffs perfectly suited to her restless mood.

Once they disembarked and started to walk, he took her hand in his. 'How are you feeling?'

'Edgy, terrified. Wondering if I've done the right thing, whether I should have let it lie. Do I really need any answers? She left me. What else do I need to know?'

A shadow crossed his face and she thought she felt him flinch but when he spoke his voice was even. 'I think knowing the answers may help give insight into why she did what she did. But there is a possibility you may not like the answers you get. So, you need to remember something.'

She looked at him, a question in her eyes, and he came to a halt, turned her so she faced him and took both her hands in his.

'That whatever or whoever she is doesn't impact on you. It doesn't add or take away from who you are. You are *not* tainted by her blood. Or your father's. They may have brought about your existence but you have made your character and you have done a wonderful job. You're strong, courageous; you've shown incredible resilience and initiative. You chose to love and protect your sister and your stepmother instead of resenting them. You care about your country and its people. Whatever you find out, whatever the answers are, cannot take away from the wonderful person you are.'

Tears moistened her eyes as she met his

gaze, saw, *felt* his sincerity, and warmth blossomed inside her.

'And if you change your mind, decide not to see her, that is okay too. It won't change the person you are.'

'Yes, it will. It will mean I'm too much of a coward to face the truth. Whatever I find out, at least it will be my mother's version, not my father's. Otherwise, I will never know why she left me. How she could have left me to live my life with a man like my father.'

Now she was sure he flinched, but his voice was gentle, as by tacit consent they sat down on the sun-warmed beach. 'I don't know what your mother was thinking but perhaps she thought it was unfair to take you from a life of wealth, take you from your birthright, your country. Especially if she was going to resume a normal life, a life without wealth, without royal trappings. Or perhaps she had no idea what she was running to, her family may not have been supportive of her leaving your father. Maybe she thought that leaving you behind was the best thing she could do for you.'

'Do you think that's possible?'

'Yes. I believe when it is your child's happiness at stake you sometimes have to make incredibly difficult decisions that it is hard for others to understand.'

'Even leaving a child.'

'Even that,' he said quietly. 'I know that's true. Because in a sense it's a decision I made myself.'

She stilled now, studied his face, saw his eyes cloud with a sadness that twisted her heart. But he met her gaze steadily. 'A few years ago, I thought I had a son.'

'I don't understand.' But she sensed he was telling her because he thought it would help her, instinctively knew that what he was about to share was deeply significant. She moved closer to him, hoped her warmth, her proximity, would help him as his had helped her.

'I met Leila when I was twenty-two, at a friend's house. She told me that she'd had an acrimonious split with her partner, that he'd been unfaithful, and then he'd thrown her out of the house they shared. I felt sorry for her and when she asked if I had a spare room she could rent I agreed.

'She moved in and very soon after that she offered to cook me a meal, to say thank you. The wine flowed and we ended up sleeping together; the next morning we both agreed it was nothing more than a mutually enjoyable one-night stand and we could easily continue to be flatmates. A few weeks later she told me she was pregnant.'

Sofia narrowed her eyes; she could see where this was going, but she couldn't believe anyone could be so duplicitous.

'At first, I was horrified. I wasn't planning on having children, and certainly not in these circumstances, but then…then I realised that how *I* felt wasn't relevant, it was the baby that mattered. Once I understood that, it felt miraculous that I was going to be a father. It was intoxicating, exhilarating and I vowed I would be the best father I could be. Leila and I decided to focus on being parents, to stay living together so I could help, could be part of the whole journey. I went to all the antenatal classes, supported Leila as much as I could through the pregnancy. I can still remember the first time I felt the baby kick. Then Leo was born and it was the most incredible moment of my life, the idea that this precious tiny newborn was my child, my son.

'The next six months were a time of wonder and awe and I felt so grateful to Leila for agreeing to us joint parenting that I didn't see what was happening. I did notice she seemed different, that she actively discouraged my parents from visiting or being involved with Leo. But I put it down to tiredness, tried to help more. Then one day when Leo was six months old, she told me the truth. Leo wasn't mine. She'd already been pregnant when we met, the whole thing was a set-up. She'd fed me a sob story, orchestrated the one-night stand and then told me I was the father.' He kept his voice even but Sofia wasn't fooled, couldn't even begin to imagine the extent of the shock and devastation Leila's news must have caused.

'Oh, Marco. That's… I'm so, so very sorry. I don't know how she could have done that.'

'She wanted Leo to have a father. A good father. She did it for him because she truly believed the real father, the birth father, would never come good. She wanted what was best for her baby.'

'But that isn't right.'

'No,' he agreed. 'But to Leila it was justifiable. But then the real father contacted her, said he had changed, and to cut a long story short he had.' Sofia knew that there was no way Marco would have let Leo go to a man who didn't check out. 'In the end they got back together and they moved with Leo to Australia. Leila told me I was "off the hook".'

'But I didn't want to be off the hook. It didn't matter to me whose blood was in Leo's veins, what his DNA was made of. To me he was mine. I'd bonded with him, loved him, changed his nappies, watched his first smile, sat up with him at night. He *was* part of me. I wanted to stay in his life, wanted him to stay in mine.'

'But you didn't stay,' she said, her heart wrenching at the enormity of the decision he must have made.

'I didn't. Because in the end I had to try to make the best decision for Leo. If his real father had been a bad person, I would have fought tooth and nail. But he wasn't. Leila admitted she'd made up a lot, exaggerated his faults. I met him, I saw him with Leo. He loved him. So how could I fight for Leo, put him in the middle of me and his real dad? He was only six months old, I knew he would forget me soon enough.'

'But *you* haven't forgotten him,' she said.

'No. And I am sure your mother hasn't forgotten you. She may well spend every day wondering if she did the right thing, just like I do. There are still days when all I want to do is get on a plane and go and see him. Even though I probably wouldn't even recognise him now and he wouldn't recognise me. Leila wanted a completely clean break; said it would be creepy if she kept me posted or updated. That she doesn't want to confuse Leo. That we all had to get on with our lives. Move on. But it's not that easy and every day I question whether I made the right decision.'

Sofia could hear the agony in his voice. So much felt clear now—how could he trust anyone when he had been so fundamentally played and betrayed? And it made it all the warmer, sweeter that he had opted to trust her. 'For what it's worth I think you did, but it must have been heartbreaking for you to do so.' And she couldn't help but wonder if it had broken her mother's heart to leave her. 'And whilst Leo may not remember who you are, what you did for him would have made a monumental difference to his life. You gave him love and security in the first months of his life, and I know you can't regret that. But I am so sorry for what happened.'

'Thank you. I know I need to move on, let it go.'

'I'm not sure that's possible. Leo will always be part of you and maybe it's okay to hold onto that little baby and carry him as a precious memory. But it must be so hard to accept what happened, come to terms with the loss.' She hesitated as an idea came to her and she looked round, saw that there was a stretch of sand near them. 'I know you said your creativity is gone and I understand that. But might it help to make a sand sculpture? Here and now. Try to put all your emotions into the sand and then the tide will take it away.'

There was a silence and she wondered if she'd overstepped. 'Only if you want to,' she said.

Did he want to? To his own surprise Marco realised he did. He'd only shared his story because he'd wanted to help Sofia, hoped it would make the next hours easier, hoped it would make the meeting with her mother a better one. But talking about Leo, seeing the way she'd listened, had seemed to ease a weight inside him. By allowing some of the buried emotions up, by reliving the past, he had seen the precious parts as well. The love he'd had for Leo, a vision of Leo's nursery with the baby mobiles hanging over the cot. How much Leo had loved them, the way he'd kicked his legs and waved his hands as they'd spun round. The first time Leo had smiled at him. The way he'd splashed in the bath. They were precious memories and maybe he should hold them close to his heart.

And as he looked at the stretch of sand, the waves lapping the shoreline, he realised that he did want to make something. Nothing permanent, but something, something that would remind him of the joy Leo had brought him.

Rising to his feet, he held out a hand, she placed hers in his and he felt a fizz, a connection, a bond as he pulled her to her feet. 'We're going to make a butterfly,' he said, hoping that her nervous energy could be allayed by the activity, that it would serve as a distraction from her upcoming meeting with her mother. That this could help both of them. 'It was Leo's favourite baby mobile. Four butterflies that went round and round in the breeze.'

'Tell me what to do and I'll help.'

Marco examined the contents of the rucksack and nodded. 'Right, we have cups, a bottle, and even a straw. Cutlery and a bowl-shaped container. They will all be useful and then the key is having wet sand. We'll make a foundation. Then we build up layers and work from the top down.'

'That sounds like a plan. I'm happy to dig and carry and try to keep the sand wet. Other than that I think my talent lies in sketching.'

'That works,' he said, his mind suddenly busy with the idea of how to use the materials at hand with the vision he had. A way to make clumps of wet sand look like something light and fragile, something that could take flight.

After that time seemed to blur; through it all he was aware of Sofia, of her grace, her ability to do exactly what she had said she would do. Her sheer presence offered a comfort, alongside her instinctive ability not to intrude. She rarely spoke, apart from the occasional question, and after a while they worked in tandem until she unobtrusively slipped away, took her sketchbook out and left him to it.

He had no idea how long he took but finally he was satisfied, stepped back and looked at what he had created.

Sofia came and stood next to him and caught her breath. 'It's…it's beautiful,' she said softly. 'How have you made it look so delicate? And its wings, the patterns, they're so simple and yet so intricate. Somehow, I can see the mobile fluttering in the breeze.' She moved closer to him. 'I can see how much you loved him.'

'I did,' he said softly. 'And you're right. I can't regret that. However much Leila's betrayal hurt me it wasn't Leo who was to blame and he gave me so much joy.' A joy that outweighed the misery. Maybe that was how his parents had felt about him. 'Thank you,' he said softly and as they stood in the late afternoon sunshine, he felt a warmth tug at his heart.

A warmth that perhaps he should step away from but right now he didn't want to. Right now, he wanted to let himself believe in an impossible dream, that somehow this was sustainable, that this moment, all the moments of the last few days, could be prolonged.

And now as he thought of baby Leo, he

hoped with all his heart that Leo was thriving
and happy and loved and suddenly, off the back
of that, another thought slipped in. Caused him
to freeze as the image seemed to go from fuzzy
to clear. Sofia and himself, standing together
and in Sofia's arms was a baby, a small dark-
haired scrap, with clear blue eyes. Their baby.
Both of them gazing down at the infant with
love.

He allowed himself to linger on the image
until reality pervaded and, with a sense of sadness, a regret that pierced, he let it go, dissolve
into the shimmering haze of sea and sunshine.

Sofia's position, her identity, her destiny
were in her own country, in Palosia. And fundamentally he knew love was not for him, knew
he'd never risk watching something beautiful
wither and rot, would never put himself in the
position his parents had put themselves into.
Could never risk the emotional fallout that parenthood could bring.

But what he could do was be here for Sofia
today, through the next hours and beyond, for
the aftermath from meeting her mother. Admiration surged through him at her courage
in facing this and he hoped she would get the
answers she wanted.

'We should get going,' he said and she nodded, gripped his hand tighter.

'It's going to be okay,' he said softly.

'Thank you for finding her, for making this happen and for being there.'

'I'm not going anywhere.' The words seemed to reverberate around them, an echo of her words earlier that morning, an intimation of commitment and, just as Sofia had earlier, he hurried to reverse them. 'I'll be waiting right outside the room, and if you need me, just call.'

CHAPTER THIRTEEN

AS THEY APPROACHED the solicitor's offices Sofia could feel her heart hammer her chest, looked up at Marco and he smiled. A smile that exuded such reassurance she felt a semblance of confidence build inside her.

He squeezed her hand. 'It *will* be okay,' he said. 'No matter what.'

They entered the building and were greeted by a receptionist. 'Your appointment is through here.'

'I'll be in the next room,' Marco said and she nodded, and as he walked away she kept her eyes on the breadth of his back. Reminded herself of all the words he had said on the beach, assembled them almost like armour before turning to follow the receptionist.

Heart in her mouth, she entered the meeting room, and came to a halt as the woman sitting at the rectangular mahogany table rose to her feet.

A woman a little bit smaller than Sofia herself, with a cascade of dark hair sprinkled with a few strands of grey. Dark blue eyes, oh, so similar to her own met hers and Sofia stood, stock-still, as the mother of her memories and dreams merged into the woman standing in front of her.

'Sofia?' The words were a whisper and her mother stepped towards her, then stopped, reached a hand out and dropped it, her eyes not wavering from her daughter's face. 'I can't believe it's really you. I have thought about this, dreamt about this.' Her voice cracked and she broke off. 'I'm sorry. I know how inadequate that sounds, that a word does not make up for anything, but I *am* sorry.'

Sofia saw the tears in her mother's eyes, saw Flavia blink them back as she went to sit down. 'I owe you an explanation,' her mother said and finally Sofia found her voice.

'I'd like that.'

The older woman sat down and Sofia followed suit, waited as Flavia visibly gathered herself together, tucked a tendril of hair behind her ear.

'I want you to know that I did love you, so very much, but I struggled. Not with you, never with you, but after the birth I felt so much weaker, so much more vulnerable because now your father had more leverage against me. He used my love for you, would taunt me with the power he had over both of us. That he could divorce me, cast me off, keep you from me and it wore me down.'

Sofia heard the weariness in her mother's tone and, knowing King Fiero as she did, she could picture the scenes, oh, so clearly, see the vindictive triumph on her father's face, and impulsively she reached out and touched her mother's arms. 'It's okay. I understand.'

'In the end…I knew I had to leave. I couldn't think straight; all I could see was a life ahead of me where he would use my love for you and yours for me as a weapon, a tool to grind us both down.' Her mother gave a smile. 'And already even when you were so little you had so much spirit, you were already trying to protect me, and the idea of watching that spirit being broken was too much. Everything became too much; life almost didn't seem worth living, but I knew I could never leave you.'

'Yet you did.' Sofia regretted the words even as she said them, saw her mother flinch. 'I'm sorry. I…'

'No. You are right. And I am not trying to make excuses. I did leave, but you have to believe me when I say I never thought I would never see you again. My plan was to leave, make sure I had somewhere for you and me to live and then I would fight for you, for custody. But I couldn't take you with me, not away from wealth and position and security. From your birthright. Not when I didn't know if my family would take me in, or where I would end up. But your father banished me. He made a case that I was an unfit mother—I was told the best I would get was occasional visitation rights. Your father told me that if I backed off, agreed not to see you again, he would not take out his anger with me on you. He would make sure you were looked after. I agreed. I know how weak that sounds, but I was weak. And every day since then, Sofia, I have wished I could turn the clock back, wished I'd made different decisions, that I'd taken you with me.'

'No.' Sofia shook her head, could see the anguish on her mother's face, knew it was genuine. She remembered Marco's anguished expression when he'd spoken of letting Leo go. 'You were in an impossible position. And you made the decisions that felt like the best thing at the time. You don't know what would have happened if you had taken me. You may have been caught and then I am sure my father would have separated us, would have kept you in Palosia and that wouldn't have benefited either of us.' She reached out again and this time she kept her hand on her mother's arm. 'I understand why you did what you did and I truly hope that the years have been good for you, that you have found happiness.'

'I have.' Her mother gave a small smile. 'Perhaps more than I deserved. I married the man I left for your father. His name is Pietro and he is…kind and gentle, yet he has an inner strength and character that make him a true prince.' Sofia could see her mother's face light up and suddenly an image of Marco filled her mind, his chivalry and strength, and she blinked it away.

'My prince. I love him…and he loves me. I should never have left Pietro; marrying your father was wrong. I did not lie to Fiero but still, what I did was wrong. I didn't understand what it would mean to marry one man whilst loving another, didn't understand the grief, the regrets. Didn't understand how difficult it would be to be touched by someone else when you knew what the act of true love felt like. But no matter what, I cannot regret you, Sofia. I have always cherished the memories I have of my time with you.'

Her mother's heartfelt words warmed her even as she imagined the true horror her marriage must have been. 'Can you tell me about those memories?' she asked, wanting to take away a true picture of her early years, wanting to be able to carry the knowledge of the time she had had with the woman who had given birth to her.

'Of course. I would love to.' Now Flavia smiled, a small sweet smile. 'Now and, I hope, in the future.'

The words were a reminder of reality. 'I hope so too but I cannot guarantee that.'

Flavia nodded, resignation writ large on her face, a face so uncannily like Sofia's own. 'I understand. Then let us make the most of the time we have now.'

Marco looked around the walls of the small waiting room for the umpteenth time and then resumed pacing, his mind concentrated on Sofia and what was happening next door, half of him wanting to simply go in and see she was all right, the other half knowing he had no right to do anything of the sort. Knowing too that Sofia had the inner strength to deal with this, that this was precious time for mother and daughter to spend together.

The thought was a reminder that after this Sofia would be free to return to Palosia. But that was not a thought for now. It was not a time to worry about the bleakness that it brought. For now, Marco simply wanted to be there for Sofia when she came out, to hold her, give comfort if needed or celebrate or listen.

It was two more hours before there was a gentle knock on the door and then Sofia came in; he could see traces of tears on her cheeks and he moved over and took her in his arms, held her close as he rubbed her back until, finally, she half pulled away, though her hands remained on his forearms.

'I'm all right,' she said. 'It was… I… I want to tell you about it, but…'

'First let's go back home. Back to the villa,' he amended quickly. 'I'll call a taxi. Then when we're back, I'll run you a bath, give you a glass of wine and then I am going to cook you the best pasta you have ever tasted. Then, if you want, you can tell me what happened.'

'That sounds perfect.'

They sat close together in the taxi, hands interlinked, the silence natural and every so often she would lightly increase the pressure of her grasp. Once back he carried out his promise, ran a bath, poured in essential oils, brought her a glass of chilled white wine and headed to the kitchen.

Forty-five minutes later the kitchen door opened and Sofia walked in. Dressed in leggings and one of his T shirts, her hair damp, her face flushed from the heat of the bath, she looked so beautiful his heart twisted.

'Perfect timing,' he said. 'I'll put the pasta in.'

'It smells incredible.'

'I thought I'd keep it simple. I made *lo spaghetto al pomodoro*. Just tomatoes, salt, fresh basil and really good olive oil. Some people say put garlic in, but I think that overpowers the overall taste, so providing I've got really good fresh tomatoes I make it without.' He was talking to distract her, could see the still shell-shocked look in her eyes.

'Thank you.' She looked a little surprised. 'Actually, I am ravenous. I guess emotion makes you hungry.'

Minutes later he placed the steaming bowls on the table along with some freshly grated *Parmigiano Reggiano*, watched with satisfaction as she started to eat, saw a bit of colour return to her cheeks.

'This really is the best pasta I've ever eaten,' she said.

'I'm glad.'

After a few moments she glanced across at him, sipped her wine. 'I'm ready to tell you now. If that's okay?'

'Of course it is. But only if you want to.' He

didn't want to force her to talk when he knew her emotions must be in overload.

'I do. It will make it feel real, rather than a dream.'

'Then I'd like to know what happened.'

She looked down at her bowl and then back up at him. 'It was almost surreal. I could see myself in her. In ways that shouldn't be possible. The way she tucks her hair behind her ear, the way she creases her forehead in thought.' She sipped her wine. 'She told me she was sorry, and she explained why she left, why she didn't fight for me. My parents' marriage was one of inequality, a marriage where my father's "love" turned to vindictive hate.'

She reached out and touched his hand. 'I know your parents' love died but at least they were united in their love for you. My father used my mother's love for me as a weapon to threaten her with. In the end she had no real choice but to leave and once she was gone, he made sure that she never saw me again. She did try but, in the end, she gave up the fight because she believed it was the best thing for me. But she has never really forgiven herself. All I could do was tell her that I forgave her. That I understood.'

His heart twisted at her understanding, her compassion, her sheer generosity of spirit.

'Do you understand?' he asked gently. 'I know how very much it has hurt all these years.'

'I think perhaps I still can't fully comprehend that it wasn't possible to fight more, fight harder, or to try to take me with her. But I do understand that she was scared and alone. My father took advantage of that vulnerability. Bullied her, broke her spirit.'

In a way he had never managed to break Sofia's and again admiration swelled in Marco.

'I can see why it was easier to start a new life here and she has. And I am truly happy for her. She married her old love, Pietro, and I could see how much she loves him. She glows when she mentions him and from what she said it is a reciprocal love. They have a son and a daughter. So, I have two more half-siblings.' Her voice held shock and question and perhaps a touch of sadness that he understood. These were siblings who had grown up with their mother. 'They live a simple life and they are happy. But there has never been a day where she hasn't thought of me.'

Her eyes welled up with tears and he moved round the table, put his arm around her. 'That is a lot to take on board. You must be feeling overwhelmed.'

'I am. Overwhelmed and dazed. I've dreamt

about meeting her for so long. Now I have and I know that she isn't a bad person. I know her reasons for leaving. But there is so much to process, to think about and I'm…'

'Exhausted,' he said, seeing the tiredness in her eyes, hearing it in her voice. 'Come on. We're going to bed.'

And that night, once they climbed into bed, he pulled her into his arms, her head on his chest, and he held her until she fell asleep, entwined in his arms, close to his heart. Until finally he fell into a deep dreamless sleep.

Sofia opened her eyes, aware that something must have awoken her but unsure of what. Remained completely still, revelled in the sense of cocooned warmth, the safety of Marco's arms around her. Then she heard it again: the buzz of her phone, notification of a message.

She glanced at Marco, saw him stir slightly and gently she eased out of his clasp, breath held, not wanting to awaken him. The only person who could be messaging her, who had this number, was Rosa. Moving as quietly as possible, she sat up, picked her phone up and tiptoed from the room, headed to the kitchen and made her way to the window enclosure.

She glanced out at the pink-tinged sky that heralded the dawn and the coming of another day. Then, taking a deep breath, she looked down, started to read.

Dearest Sofia
Father has found you and he is so very furious. He had a guard following your mother, and that led him to you. I am not sure what he will do next.
Belle

Sofia felt the hammer of her heart against her ribs, her ears already alert for the knock at the door, the inevitable tread of the guards' footsteps. She forced her brain to think. The phone was a new number but both the signature and the code words indicated the messages were genuinely from her sister. In which case her father could have sent the guards the night before. Presumably he was holding fire, wouldn't want to create a scandal. Marco's wealth and position might also play a part in causing King Fiero to at least pause for thought. She returned her attention to her phone, the next instalment.

Eduardo has now stated that he no longer wishes to marry you. He is going to marry Luciana. Father has a plan. You are to return home and continue the pretence of illness. Then in two months you will release Eduardo from his engagement. A few months later you will get engaged to Count Arturion. Father has arranged the marriage.

Sending you so very much love
Belle

Panic cascaded over her, and she half rose from the chair. All of her wanting, needing, to go to Marco, to wrap herself around him and beg him to never let her go. She forced herself to remain still, told herself not to be foolish.

She had known, they had both known, this would happen. That she would have to return. That her destiny, her duty, lay in an arranged marriage. This interlude had always had an end date baked in.

But all those words, all the logic in the world did nothing to stem the sheer force of the denial rising in her, the soaring sense of despair evoked at the idea of being wrenched away from the man she loved.

Whoa. Stop the press.

The man she what?

Now images of Marco streamed through her mind, his touch, his smile, his scent, his warmth, his chivalry. The way her heart hopped, skipped and jumped at the sight of him, the sense of safety and security he engendered. How he made her laugh, the way his smile caused her heart to leap. She blinked the images away, but however hard she tried to block the knowledge, to dodge the bullet, she couldn't. The truth was blinding in its horrible crystal clarity. She loved him, heart, body and soul.

What was she going to do?

Her phone beeped again and she looked down at the next message.

Saw that it was from her father, or at least issued by the authority of King Fiero.

Sofia, I have discovered your whereabouts. I will give you two choices. To present yourself at the ferry port before eleven a.m. today. Or I will take matters in my own hands.

Sofia glanced at her watch. There was time. But time for what? She had no doubt there was a guard posted within sight of the villa. There could be no escape. Plus, where would she be escaping to? What would she be escaping from now? The only option was to return to Palosia.

She couldn't stay here, could never tell Marco of her love. They had undertaken this interlude on the basis of a mutual rejection of love. The terms absolute. She wouldn't, couldn't admit to Marco that she loved him, wouldn't do that to him. It would feel as if she had somehow betrayed his trust; he'd believed her to be immune to love, believed this interlude was safe.

Marco did not want her love. And he would hate the idea of hurting her, of inflicting pain.

There was no more time. Their time was up. Duty in the shape of Count Arturion summoned her. The thought shattered her; her heart was slowly breaking into pieces. The idea of leaving Marco caused a sear of pain nigh on impossible to bear. But somehow, she had to, because anything else was truly impossible.

How would she say goodbye? How would she hide her feelings from Marco? For a craven moment Sofia looked at the door. Perhaps the best thing for them both would be if she simply left. But could she leave without seeing him one last time?

CHAPTER FOURTEEN

MARCO OPENED HIS EYES, intensely aware that something was missing, that the bed next to him was empty, and when he stretched a hand out the sheets were cool to the touch.

His heart seemed to skip a beat as a sudden sense of panic, of history repeating, assailed him. No, Sofia wouldn't, couldn't, have gone. Couldn't have been spirited away by palace guards whilst he slept through. But the foreboding, dread, sheer panic, wouldn't abate, scrambled all his senses. The idea that she could be gone from his life caused a wrenching sense of loss, made his feelings of seven years before pale in comparison.

As he tugged a pair of jeans on, stumbling in his haste, all he could envisage was the sight of an empty house, and the desolation that would come with it. His brain tried to figure out a plan, work out timings, when it could have happened, what he was going to do. He wasn't ready for her to go. Not yet. There must be a way to circumvent the guards, keep her in his life for longer, to stay in hers. But what if Sofia didn't want that? The question was like an icy deluge of doubt. What if this time she'd chosen to go completely voluntarily?

A few strides later and he registered the smell of coffee. Hope surged as he shoved the kitchen door open with precipitate haste, and relief washed over him as he saw her.

'I… I'm glad you're here. I thought maybe… you'd gone.'

Wariness touched her expression. 'I'm here. I haven't disappeared without leaving a note. Not this time.'

He studied her face, saw its pallor in the early morning sunshine, her eyes smudged with sadness. 'But something has happened,' he said as foreboding unfurled anew in his gut.

She took a deep breath. 'Yes.'

'Are you leaving?' The question jerked out of him, in the desperate hope of reassurance, but somehow the hope already felt doomed. Her expression held the answer. He could see it in her eyes even before she inclined her head.

'Yes. This past week has been…incredible, magical; the type of week I never thought was possible for me,' she said. 'But it can't go on for ever. For either of us.'

Why not? He bit the words back, knew she was right. There could be no for ever for them.

'But why go now?' Why would she want to leave when she had just found her mother, when she was still in the midst of working on the villa, when they were happy together, dammit?

Now her composure seemed rattled and she cupped her hands round her cup of coffee as if for comfort. 'I got a message. Early this morning. From Rosa.'

The foreboding deepened. 'What did it say?'

'My father has found me. He set a guard on my mother. He is furious and I suppose I can see why. If you and I become public my reputation will be ruined. He has demanded my immediate return.'

'What about Eduardo?'

'That is over; Eduardo is going to marry the woman he loves.' Her face lightened slightly. 'I am glad for him. But my father has another plan.'

He waited, saw her hands clench into fists, and he reached out and covered her hand in his. She looked down, briefly covered his hand with her own and then gently pulled back.

'In about six months' time I will marry someone else.'

Now his own fists clenched and he had to force himself to remain still. 'Who?'

'A Palosian aristocrat. He is a massive land-owner, owns a huge number of olive groves and he will agree to enter into business with the Crown. In return for my hand in marriage. I know him. He is a good man; he will understand that I have had a previous relationship. But he will not want it to be made public. So it is imperative that no one finds out about us, that we are not seen together. I have to go back. There is no other choice.'

Marco stared at her, his whole mind, his whole body rejecting this idea. Rejecting everything. 'There is always another choice,' he said flatly.

'Not in this case.' Her gaze met his. 'I've already taken too many risks. Realistically at some point someone will recognise either you or me. Then what? Then my marriage prospects are in tatters. I truly don't regret any decision I have made so far; I don't regret my time with you. How could I?' Her voice caught. 'This interlude has been magical. But it has to end here. Before there are any regrets. Before I bring disgrace to my name, prove my father right, demonstrate that I am truly no princess. I don't want misery to outweigh the joy you have brought me. Do you see that?'

'Yes.' That was the worst of it. He did. Understood the importance of her royal duties and obligations, her loyalty to her country and her sister. What could he offer against that?

But there had to be another choice. There had to be. Now he started to pace, desperation triggering ideas, assessing and discarding, until… 'There is another choice, another option,' he said, coming to a halt in front of her. 'Marry me,' he said.

Sofia stared at him as the silence stretched.

'Excuse me?' she said, deciding that her tired, distraught brain must have misheard him. Ever since she'd received Rosa's messages, her mind had been in turmoil. But now, now Marco had thrown a bombshell into her thought process. Her heart leapt, tumbled, flipped as she looked at him.

'Marry me,' he repeated and now his voice was firmer, filled with confidence. 'An arranged marriage with me instead of with a Palosian aristocrat or a prince. I know that I don't have blue blood in my veins, but I do have a lot of money. I am sure I can come to some sort of deal with your father. I could invest in Palosia. In olive oil. In perfumes. You mentioned that Chiara has set up a successful hat business. I could help expand that further, increase exports. Use my platform to help market Palosian goods. We could live on Palosia some of the year and abroad the rest. You'd have your freedom. We wouldn't have to live in each other's pockets. You could go where you wanted whenever you wanted. You could train as an interior designer, still see Rosa.'

His words painted such a beautiful picture, one so full of allure, that she could almost taste the happiness it would bring. A place on Palosia, walking the oak-lined avenue in the palace gardens with Rosa, hand in hand with Marco leading him through, or better yet getting lost in, the twist and turns of the verdant green walls of the palace maze. A house in Italy, an office in an interior-design firm and, in every scene, Marco was by her side. She blinked, tried to think, really think. Marco was offering an arranged marriage, in which case—

'But what do *you* get from this?'

'Any deal I negotiate with your father will benefit Krafty. On a personal note, I'd gain a relationship I can navigate. Because otherwise what are my alternatives? A series of potential short-term affairs, always seeking a woman who truly doesn't believe in love? Always feeling uncomfortable. Always worried I'll hurt someone. Or you and I can get married. An extension of our interlude, a relationship that can't turn bitter or sour because neither side wants or believes in love.

'You told me all the benefits of an arranged marriage, security, liking, respect. We have all that and we also have trust and attraction thrown in. I know you want a family and I believe we could make that work as well. We would both be truly committed to parenthood and we would also be a unit, offering our children security and stability. And if for some reason our marriage doesn't work then at least we would be able to work out an amicable agreement where we put our children first. We wouldn't be locked into a destructive cycle like my parents. I think this could work for both of us.'

And for one glorious moment Sofia believed it could. Imagined being with Marco all the time, having a baby, *their* baby… Marco cradling the tiny infant, looking down with love in his eyes and herself looking on at the man she loved.

The thought pulled her up short. And the full irony, the horror of the situation burst upon her as she stared at Marco, took in the, oh, so familiar features, the face that she'd seen smile, laugh and frown. The face that had looked on her with compassion, caring, desire… But never love. Because he didn't believe in love.

Because he didn't love her. However much she loved him. And in falling in love with him, she'd wrecked everything.

Because she couldn't marry him. Couldn't enter a marriage that was one-sided, though for a deluded moment she'd told herself that she could. That she could hide her love.

Such futile reasoning, which she knew to be wrong. Knew she had to find the resolution to do the right thing. He'd made it plain that the basis of the arrangement, the only reason he was contemplating it, was that he believed she didn't love him. Trusted her to be entering the deal on that basis. She couldn't betray that trust, knew it would make for a marriage of misery, with her hoping every day, every night, that she might make him love her. And you couldn't. You couldn't make people love you. A one-sided marriage couldn't work.

It was only now that the penny dropped and the full ramifications of her foolishness dawned on her. She wouldn't be able to marry Count Arturian whilst knowing she loved Marco. Because a marriage couldn't work if one person loved someone else. That was why she hadn't married Eduardo. Her mother's words echoed in her head. *I didn't understand what it would mean to marry one man whilst loving another, didn't understand the grief,*

*the regrets. Didn't understand how difficult it
would be to be touched by someone else when
you knew what the act of true love felt like…*

How had she let this happen? So blithely believed she could embark on this interlude and
move on? How ridiculous her reasoning felt
now. And now…now Marco was waiting for
an answer. And even as she heard the crack of
her heart, knew she might well spend the rest
of her life ruing and regretting this decision,
still she knew it was the only thing to do.

'I can't marry you,' she said, keeping her
voice even.

'Why not?' His lips set in a grim line.

'Because it wouldn't work,' she said, realising as she said the words that they were the
truth. This wasn't only about her; it was also
about him. 'You deserve more than to get embroiled in my family's political and emotional
messes. All you wanted was an interlude, you
don't really want marriage. Or a family.'

Now she could see why he'd made the offer.
'You are trying to do what you have always
done. Protect me. But providing me with sanctuary for a week is one thing, committing
yourself to a marriage you don't truly want is
another. So, thank you from the bottom of my
heart, but I can't marry you. So, the sooner
I leave, the better.' She knew she couldn't

hold it together for much longer. Knew every second she remained with him it would become harder and harder to stick to her resolve. To do what she knew to be right. 'My father has told me I can meet a Palosian escort at the ferry. They will have organised a discreet return to Palosia.' She rose to her feet.

'Sofia, wait. I… I didn't make the offer lightly. Please believe that.'

'I do. But I can't bear the thought of you regretting it. You said to me that you didn't believe that any long-term relationship, arranged or not, can work, because there are no guarantees. That you don't want commitment and you don't think it's fair to risk bringing a child into that or even fair to enter any relationship. I can't and won't have children with someone who is only having a family for me. You can't extend an interlude into a marriage—there are different rules and expectations.' She stepped towards him. 'I truly wish you nothing but happiness and I will never forget our interlude. Not ever. I'll call a taxi.' She pulled out her phone and quickly did that.

'But before I go, I need to give you this.' She placed the sketchbook on the table. 'This has proposed sketches for all the rooms and there are more detailed plans on your laptop, along with suggested outlets and sources.'

'Thank you.' She saw the sadness on his face, and it wrung her heart.

'I'll wait outside.'

'I'll come out.'

She shook her head. 'No. It will be easier if you don't. No one will think twice about your interior decorator getting in a taxi to leave. Job done.'

And indeed, it was. Sofia willed herself not to cry, allowed herself one last touch, one hand placed on his forearm, on the lithe swell of muscles, one hand to cup his jaw with its morning shadow. A light brush of her lips on his cheek—she didn't dare do more. Already his proximity threatened to shatter her fragile resolution.

'Goodbye, Marco. Thank you for all you have done for me and I will follow your next steps. It's better if we don't stay in touch.'

He inclined his head and she saw his hands clench by his sides as if he was preventing himself from even lifting a hand, and she was grateful for that restraint.

'Goodbye, Sofia. I hope, I wish, that all your dreams come true. I know you will be a wonderful parent and I hope your father appreciates what you are doing, sees your true worth and beauty. You are a true princess. Not because of who you marry but because of who you are.'

She knew she had to go now, that instant, before it was no longer possible for her to do so. And as she closed the door behind her, she thought her heart might crack in two; the pain a burning sear of grief.

Three days later

Marco looked round the villa; he should have left by now but, somehow, he hadn't been able to. Staying here made him feel closer to Sofia. He'd checked the Internet constantly for Palosian news, rewarded with a single photo of a 'convalescing princess', Sofia's hair no longer highlighted brown, but dyed back to its natural colour, her face pale, but at least he knew she was safe.

He sat at the kitchen table, opened the sketchbook yet again, turned to the last page and his heart turned over as he looked at the sketch, saw the words she had written.

Dear Marco
I have drawn this idea without consulting you; I hope you don't mind. However hard I try I cannot believe all your passion for your art, all your creativity, is truly gone. Please know I am not trying to take away from what you have achieved, your suc-

cess and your hard work are phenome-nal. But I think there is still some of the idealistic dreamer inside you, and I hope one day you let yourself dream again of your art.

   With all my best wishes
Sofia

He looked at the accompanying pictures, the sketch of a workshop, her handwritten notes—the detail of the picture showed how much thought she had put into it. The research into potters' wheels and forges, the maximisation of natural light, the thought for storage and space. The idea that Sofia had done this for him, that she still believed in the young man he'd once been, in a talent he had long since given up on, brought a slew of emotion. Warmth and also a frustration that all her talent displayed in this sketchbook—the combination of vision and detail—would be wasted on some landown-ing count. The thought twisted his gut with anger and a bleak, searing desolation. He rose to his feet, aware of an urge to smash some-thing, punch a wall, do something, anything, to disperse these unwanted feelings.

   The ring of the doorbell was a welcome dis-traction; it would be his mother and Lorenzo. He'd asked them to come and see the villa and he needed to at least show a good face on it. After all, this was a gift for her, a place for her and her family to come and relax, enjoy themselves.

Sofia's voice echoed in his head. 'You are her family. And this is a chance to embrace that.'

He pulled the front door open, saw his mum on the doorstep and conjured up a smile, tried to keep his voice normal. 'Just you? I thought Lorenzo was coming too.'

'He's gone for a walk round Capri. I wanted to see you on your own,' Giulia said, her gaze intent as he led the way into the kitchen. She glanced round and headed straight for the coffee machine. 'I didn't want to give you the chance to deflect questions with social inanities. Plus, I thought you may feel more comfortable speaking with just me. I know you and Lorenzo haven't really become close.'

'I...'

'But that's for another day. When I spoke to you, you sounded sad.' She handed him a cup of coffee. 'You look tired and...you look more than sad, you look desolate. Like you did after Leo.' She hesitated. 'After that happened you said you wanted to be left alone and I listened to you. I'm sorry. I was caught up with Lorenzo and, looking back now, I shouldn't have left you alone. I should have been there for you.'

'It wasn't your fault.' He meant every word. 'You did try. Both you and Dad tried. But I wanted to deal with it myself. Anyway,' he added brightly, 'a lot has happened since then. You and Lorenzo have got married, you have a lovely family and...'

His mother shook her head. 'Uh-uh. *I* am not going to be deflected. Yes, I am lucky to have Lorenzo and, yes, I get on incredibly well with his children. *His* children,' she repeated. '*You* are *my* child, *my* family. I know something is wrong and I want to help.' She reached out, touched his arm. 'I am not moving until you tell me what's happened.'

Looking at his mother's determined face, Marco could see she meant it. In truth he wanted to talk about Sofia, needed to work out how to snap out of this. Perhaps his mother could help him find perspective. 'I met someone,' he said. 'And now she's gone and I miss her. But I know I'll get over it and I know it's all for the best.'

His mother frowned slightly. 'Why? Why is it all for the best?'

'Because she didn't want to marry me. I offered her a deal but she —' He broke off at his mother's expression, her mouth agape.

'I'm a bit lost. If you proposed and she refused—that's not a deal.'

'It's complicated.'

'I'll concentrate hard.' Giulia sat at the table and he followed suit, started to explain.

Five minutes later she put her cup down. 'So let me get this straight. You met a princess who was running away from one arranged marriage, but accepted that a different arranged marriage was her destiny. She wanted a week of freedom. You helped her and in that time you and she became involved on the premise it was a temporary fling. Yet when she had to leave you offered to marry her. Why?'

'Because it made sense. I could offer her a better deal. A marriage where she would have real freedom to pursue her dreams, have a family and a career, make decisions for herself.'

His mother looked at him. 'And what was in it for you?' she asked. The same question that Sofia had asked. And suddenly Marco wasn't sure of the answer. What had he wanted, really wanted? The answer hit him. He'd wanted Sofia to stay in his life. But that wasn't the point. This was—

'It made sense. I could have a relationship without the complications of love with a woman I trusted. A relationship where, if anything went wrong, we would be able to split amicably without bitterness. Move on.'

'A marriage completely unlike mine with your father's,' she said softly. 'A marriage with safety nets and rules.'

'Yes.'

'Why did she refuse?'

'She said it wasn't fair to me. That I didn't really want marriage or children. And she couldn't have children with someone who was doing it for her.'

'Was she right?'

'No.' The answer instinctive and instant. Because there was no relief that Sofia had refused. There was only burning regret for what could now never be. Each morning of waking up brought a bleakness and a sense of emptiness at the knowledge he would never hear her voice, never hold her, or see her face light up in a smile. All he wanted to do was fly to Palosia and storm the palace to get to her.

'No,' he repeated. 'She wasn't right. I do want to marry her; I do want a family with her.' The words were so natural and brought up such vivid pictures. Sofia holding a baby, *their* baby, a little girl with a smattering of dark hair and wide blue eyes. The idea brought an upswell of feeling and he stared at his mum in a moment of breathtaking realisation. He loved Sofia.

'Because that makes sense?' his mum asked softly. 'Or for another reason?'

'I...'

'Marco, if you love her, then please, please don't walk away from that love, please don't give her up without a fight, without at least telling her the truth.'

'But... I... I don't want love. And neither does Sofia. She refused my proposal.'

'She refused your proposal of a deal, an arranged marriage. I don't know how Sofia feels about you, maybe she doesn't either. But if you love her, perhaps she deserves to know.'

Marco tried to think. Could Sofia love him? Was it possible? Looking back over the past days, he thought about the connection between them, all the confidences they had shared, how easy and relaxed and happy they had both been. Remembered holding her, remembered the passion they had shared.

'Even if we do love each other, how do I know it is sustainable, that this isn't a mirage, a temporary phase that won't survive reality? How do I know that I won't end up hurting her, or impacting our family?' The thought of bringing pain to Sofia, of seeing her beautifull face look at him with disdain or contempt, was unbearable.

'You don't know. I can't give you a cast-iron guarantee,' Giulia said. 'But I can tell you all marriages aren't like mine and your father's. I am sorry, truly sorry, for what we put you through. With hindsight it was selfish of both of us. And I don't know what happened. Once I did love your father and he loved me. Maybe we didn't work hard enough at it. Love isn't always easy, it has downs as well as ups and your dad and I weren't prepared for that. We never really talked; we never really shared our feelings.

'But just because we got it wrong doesn't mean love can't work. There are no guarantees but that doesn't mean you shouldn't try. I love Lorenzo and I truly believe we will make it. I never take our love for granted and I will work at it, tend it, nurture it and, if need be, I will fight for it. I was scared to risk loving him but in the end the thought of losing him, losing the chance of love, gave me the courage to risk it.'

Marco listened and as he did, he thought of Sofia. They had trusted each other with their very souls, had taken such joy in each other, and he had tried to control that joy, put in rules and regulations and safety nets. Had offered her a deal. He gave a small groan.

'I've messed up,' he said.

'Then go and fix it.' The words were so simple but she was right. Blindingly right. He had to fix this. He loved Sofia and he had to let her know. Before it was too late and he regretted it for the rest of his life. If she didn't love him, so be it. He wanted her to know of his love for her. Wanted to give his love a chance, hoped with all his heart that she would too.

'I will. Thank you. And soon, I want to get to know Lorenzo better and his family. I am so glad you have found love and happiness.' He went and hugged her. 'Thank you again. Here are the keys. You and Lorenzo look round. I have to go.'

Palosian Palace

Sofia sat at the table in the royal bedroom, glanced out of the window, tried to find some solace or tranquillity from the palace gardens, but the bloom and beauty of the terraced flower beds couldn't permeate her fogged senses. The whole world seemed tinged in ash grey, the colour of her crumbled dreams and hopes.

She looked back down at her open sketchbook; drawing had been the only thing to offer peace in the past bleak days. Sketches of Marco. Pictures of Capri, images so indelibly etched on her mind, her heart, her very soul. Memories she knew she would treasure for ever even as she somehow worked out how to rebuild her life. Once the pain, the grief, the desolation of missing Marco eased, each night an escape into dreams of a different life, dreams where he was lying next to her. Only to awake in the morning to the flower-scented breeze from the palace gardens and the dreary, inescapable knowledge that Marco was not there.

A knock on the door heralded the arrival of Rosa and Sofia gently closed the sketchbook, not ready to share the images even with Rosa.

'I came to see how you are feeling,' Rosa said, entering the room with her soft tread, her face full of compassion and love. 'I can sense your sadness.'

How to answer that question? How was she feeling? Heartbroken. Devastated. Furious with herself for the folly of falling in love. Full of the ache of missing Marco.

'Or perhaps it would be better for me to ask what happened. Something happened to you in Naples. You look different. You are different.'

Sofia looked at her sister, tried to decide what she should do. Could she confide in Rosa? Rosa who had her own arranged marriage to deal with at some point in time. With all the added pressure of producing an heir to contend with.

As if sensing her thoughts, Rosa stepped forward, sat opposite her. 'You can talk to me, Sofia. I want to help.'

Sofia looked at Rosa's beautiful face, her eyes wide and sympathetic, and she realised Rosa was right. 'I am different,' she said softly. 'I fell in love, and it has changed everything. How I look at the world. It was one of the most foolish things I could have done, but I did it anyway.'

'And you regret it?' Rosa asked, wonder and genuine curiosity in her words. 'I know we princesses are not supposed to look for love, whatever the fairy tales say, but do you truly regret it?'

Sofia opened her mouth and closed it again, considered the question. If she could turn time back, would she change anything, forgo the pleasure, the joy, the laughter, the companionship? To never experience any of that would make her world a darker place. Yes, now all she felt was the pain, loss and grief of love unrequited. But being with Marco, experiencing love, had changed her, changed her whole life and given it a new perspective.

'I don't know,' she admitted. 'Perhaps it

would feel different if he loved me back. But he doesn't.'

'How do you know? Did he say that?'

'Not explicitly, but I know. He doesn't want love, believes it isn't made to last, that when it goes wrong it causes bitterness, so you are better off without it.'

'All the things you thought until you fell in love with him,' Rosa pointed out, the gentleness of her tone underpinned with an unfamiliar edge. 'Perhaps Marco has changed his mind too.'

The thought poleaxed her.

'Are you willing to gamble your life away on the assumption that he hasn't? Plus, surely Marco deserves the truth. Surely it is good for people to know they are loved?'

'But even if he did love me, there is no future for us. Our father would never permit the marriage. He would banish me and then...'

'Then what?' Rosa said, taking a deep breath as she saw Sofia's eyes widen in surprise. 'Then you would have to leave me? All your life you have protected me. I know you have stayed here in part for me and I love you for it. But I don't want you to give up your chance of love and happiness for me. In fact, I won't have it. As for your duty to Palosia, our father took away your succession rights. You don't owe him anything.'

Sofia looked at her sister, her beautiful, kind, insightful, selfless sister who she loved so much. A love that would never wither or die. Just as her love for Marco wouldn't. Rosa was right. Marco did deserve to know he was loved and valued. And he deserved the truth from her. Withholding that truth was in itself a betrayal of trust.

As they spoke there was a ping from Rosa's phone.

Her sister's eyes widened. 'I can't quite believe this, but I think it's Marco.'

'How do you know?'

'I'm assuming you told him about our code.' Sofia nodded. 'He's signed it Mark.'

Sofia nodded, remembered she'd written Rosa's mobile number in the sketchbook she'd left with Marco. 'What does it say?'

'He wants to see you, to meet you. He says it's urgent. He will come to wherever you say.'

It could be to discuss the villa ideas, Sofia told herself. Or to discuss the arranged marriage again. Or most likely he wanted to make sure she was all right.

But whatever it was she knew what she needed to do next. She rose to her feet, leant down and gave Rosa a hug.

'Thank you. Please message him back. Tell him I will come to Naples. But now I am going to see Father.'

Rosa's eyes widened in concern. 'But wouldn't it be better to talk to Marco first? Or...'

Sofia shook her head. 'No. It is time I stood on my own two feet.'

Two days later

Marco had never felt this wracked with nerves in all his twenty-eight years, but neither had he felt such heady anticipation. Anticipation laced with dread, a fear that this really would be the last time he saw Sofia. He wasn't even sure how she had managed to leave Palosia, but she had asked him to choose a place to meet in Naples. So here he was, at the place where they had shared their very first kiss seven years ago. Yet as he looked down over the panoramic sprawl of Naples, all he could think of was Sofia.

Anxiety strummed again. Perhaps she would tell him of the impending announcement of her engagement. Worse, perhaps his nightmare of the previous night would come true: Sofia would arrive with the count in tow.

Marco forced his body to relax, scanned

the people headed in his direction and his heart skipped a beat. There was Sofia. Simply dressed in one of the dresses she'd bought on Capri, a pattern of purple and blue, her dark hair now a little bit longer. Then she was next to him, slightly breathless from the steep climb, and he couldn't help the smile that tipped his lips. It was a smile that encompassed relief and happiness and she smiled back, a smile that lit her face, and they stood in a timeless moment where anything was possible, an instant of hope, a chance and infinite potential.

But then the nerves returned and he reminded himself that he had no idea of her agenda, of her reasons for agreeing to this meeting. As if mirroring his thoughts, she took a step back and her face became serious, her dark blue eyes full of both wariness and determination.

'So, who goes first?' she asked.

Perhaps he should be polite and let her, but he couldn't. He was here to fight for Sofia, to tell her how he truly felt, and he wouldn't bottle it. Not now. Not when she was standing here and his whole being was filled with his love for her, a burning desire to pull her into his arms.

'If it's all right with you, I'll go first.'

She hesitated and then nodded. 'Go ahead.'

'First I want to apologise.'

'For what?' There was genuine surprise in her voice.

'For offering you a mealy-mouthed proposal for an arranged marriage.'

Was that disappointment that crossed her blue eyes, before she blinked it away?

'You were offering me way more than that,' she said softly. 'You were offering me freedom, an alternative to another marriage. But I completely understand that you are withdrawing that offer. I didn't come here to tell you I'd changed my mind.'

Now it was his turn to blink as he realised she'd got the wrong end of the stick, thought he'd asked to see her to rescind the proposal completely.

'I *am* withdrawing that offer. Because I want to replace it with another.' And now the nerves, the fear of rejection no longer mattered. All that mattered was telling Sofia the truth. 'Will you marry me? Not as part of a deal or an arrangement. Not out of convenience. This time I am offering you my heart, my love, my commitment for the rest of my life.'

Her eyes widened and he saw the disbelief.

'Whatever your answer is, I want you to know that I love you, Sofia. With all my heart. You've changed me, you've made me see everything differently. I've seen how you have navigated life with such strength and kindness and through it all your inner beauty shines. You shone a light in *my* life in Capri, just as you did seven years ago. You light up my world and these past days without you have been bleak. I want to wake up with you by my side for the rest of my life. If you'll have me. You don't need to answer now, please take some time, think about what I have said. I know you don't believe in love, but I promise you my love for you will not change, that it is true and real. But if you don't love me, I still won't regret loving you, because it has brought me joy.'

She stepped forward, reached up to cup his face, her blue eyes holding his gaze unwaveringly and what he saw there made his heart beat faster.

'I don't need any time to think, because the answer is simple. Of course I will marry you. I am offering you my heart, my love, my commitment for the rest of my life. I came here today to tell you that I loved you. To tell you how you have changed my life and my beliefs. You have shown me so much, how to believe in myself and my talent. To see that I can stand up to my father and stand on my own two feet and that does not make me any less of a princess. That my blood is not tainted. I have seen your strength, your resilience and your generosity. In choosing to trust me when there were so many reasons for you to have walked away. You truly are a knight in shining armour, not for protecting me, but for showing me how to protect myself. Showing me the joy of love. So yes, yes, yes! I will marry you. With all my heart.'

In that moment he felt a joy so great he didn't know how to harness it as he reached into his pocket and then went down on one knee in front of her, uncaring of the crowd they were gathering. He opened the box and, taking her left hand in his, he slipped the ring onto her finger, stood up as she held it up, over the city of Naples, so that the sun glinted off the jewels.

'It's beautiful.' She studied the ring and then looked up at him. 'Did you…?'

'Make it? Yes, I did.' To his elation the skills he'd learnt years before had still been there and in the past days he'd thrown himself into creating something he'd hoped Sofia would love. A ring with crossing bands studded with carefully selected colourful jewels interspersed with diamonds that somehow represented to him the idea of her freedom, her beauty and the way she lit up the world.

Now her smile grew even wider and she threw herself into his arms and hugged him. 'That makes it infinitely more precious. I will love looking at it every day for the rest of my life.'

The words brought another smile to his face as he contemplated the sheer happiness of spending the rest of his life with this woman, this wonderful, strong, beautiful woman. 'My creativity is back.' Triggered by her belief in him.

'I am so pleased for you,' she said. 'I know what an important part of you that is.'

'And I know the same for you. And I know how important your country and your sister are to you. We will go to your father and I will do everything in my power to make sure you are not separated from Rosa or Palosia.'

'It's okay,' she said. 'I spoke to my father before I left. I told him I would not enter an arranged marriage. I explained that my time away had changed me. That I was no longer willing to obey his every decree without question and I no longer believed that was where my duty lay. I told him I wanted to show my people that a princess can rule, can be independent and earn her own money. I told him I wanted to work for Palosia and for myself.'

Admiration filled him for the courage it must have taken. 'I wish I could have been with you.'

'In some ways it felt as though you were.

Because it was the time I spent with you that showed me it was possible to stand up to him. That and the wisdom of my sister.'

'Did your father see your point of view?'

'No.' Sofia shook her head. 'If this were a film, I suppose he would have. But he didn't. He lost the plot. He forbad me to leave, threatened to make sure I never saw Rosa again.'

'I'm sorry.'

'Don't be.' Now she smiled, a sudden impish smile. 'I said that was his prerogative. But I didn't think the people would stand for that. That I would put my case to them. That for now I was leaving Palosia to visit Naples, that I would do it honestly and openly.

'He blustered, he shouted, and he called security, but I told him that if he secured me in my room word would get out and I would go public with the truth. In the end he let me go. I don't know if he will let me back. But I hope that he will. And Rosa has given me her blessing.

'But whatever happens I needed to tell you that you are loved. And now today you have told me that you love me. From this day forward we will go forward together, and I know there may be downs as well as ups but I know we will navigate every bump in the road. Together.'

He nodded. 'And we will make sure our children have security and love and that they are brought up by two parents who love each other and them.'

She looked up at him. 'Do you mean that? I know after Leo, after your own upbringing, you may not want children. And if you don't that is truly okay. I love you. I am marrying you because I love you, not for a family, or wealth or security.'

'I know that. And I feel exactly the same. But I *want* to have children with you. I loved Leo so very much and I loved being a father and now, now I can see how wonderful it will be to bring a family up with you. You will be an amazing mother.'

'And you will be an amazing father, just like you were with Leo.'

'Maybe we will have a little girl with your dark hair.'

'And a boy with your grey eyes.'

'Or any combination, any gender, but I want to see you hold our baby. I want to go on family outings to the park. I want the chance to watch our children grow. But most of all, whatever life brings us, I want that life to be with you.'

And now seven years after their first kiss, standing above the glorious vista of Naples, the stretch of history from the ancient fourteenth-century bell tower to the towering recent sky-scrapers, he took her into his arms. And as his lips touched hers and they were bathed in the orange glow of a glorious sunset, Marco knew he was the happiest man in the universe.

EPILOGUE

Seven months later,
wedding day on Palosia

SOFIA LOOKED AT her reflection in the mirror, and both awe and wonder flooded her at the thought of the hours ahead. She was going to marry Marco. Here on Palosia. Today she would make vows committing herself to the man who she had grown to love even more over the past months. In those months Eduardo had married his Luciana, despite opposition from his family, and both he and Sofia had insisted on telling the truth. They had announced they had ended their engagement because they both loved other people. But that they would remain friends and they hoped the people would understand and forgive the scandal.

They had all agreed to interviews and between them all they had won the people over.

Sofia suspected the majority had been pleased that their royal families were moving with the times.

Marco had handled meetings with the king and courtiers with aplomb, civility and a steely strength that she knew had inspired a grudging respect from all. Even perhaps her father. And with Marco by her side, together they had negotiated a wedding on Palosia, and an agreement that, although she would have to request permission to visit, her father would consider those requests.

She turned as Rosa entered the room. 'You look stunning.'

They both said the words at the same time and exchanged a smile. One of the best parts of the wedding preparations had been choosing the bridesmaid dress with Rosa, and Sofia loved the look her sister had opted for. It was so very quintessentially Rosa. The simple high-waisted floral dress with its floaty style somehow epitomising the sheer happiness Sofia herself felt. The whole perfectly complemented by the circlet of fresh flowers woven into Rosa's silken fair hair that flowed loose around her shoulders.

'I've come to help with any last-minute preparations. And you do look stunning. Beautiful. Radiant, in fact.'

'I feel radiant,' Sofia said. And she knew it was nothing to do with her dress, though she absolutely adored it. This time the choice was truly hers, not motivated by the need to impress. Chosen simply with her love, because she wanted Marco to look at her and see her happiness, and she also wanted to knock his socks off. And she hoped the classic elegance of the dress would do exactly that. It was long-sleeved with a boat neck and made in Chantilly lace, its skirt flaring in graceful folds.

'No doubts?'

'Not a single one. I am truly floating on air. The love I feel for Marco has lit up my life. And I am so happy you are going to be my only bridesmaid.' Rosa would carry the much lighter, less ostentatious train of this gown.

'Are you all right with Father giving you away?'

'Yes. It…felt right.' Sofia didn't believe she and her father could ever be truly close, but she did feel she owed him something. He was Palosia's king and he did have the country's best interests at heart. She wouldn't invoke gossip or scandal by refusing to let him play his traditional role. On some level she appreciated King Fiero's pragmatic acceptance of the marriage even if it was motivated by Marco's wealth and position. Deep down she even still hoped that somehow, some day they could have some sort of relationship.

But regardless of that she now did have new family. In deference to Palosia's traditions she had not moved in with Marco prior to marriage, had mainly lived on Palosia for the time of their engagement. But he had spent time on Palosia and she had made trips to Italy, had met Giulia and Lorenzo and his children. Had stayed for a family holiday at the villa and it had been fun, the type of fun she and Rosa had never experienced. Family meals, board games played amid laughter and banter. Shopping trips with Marco's mother, honest, open conversations.

And Marco's dad had come to stay in Palosia, had reduced her to helpless laughter with his jokes. He had also divulged that he was pursuing a career as an artist, showed them his work, landscapes of the Scottish Highlands, and told them with pride that his work was garnering some recognition. That he had also met a fellow artist, a woman for whom he was beginning to develop feelings.

As for Flavia and her family, Sofia was in touch and after the marriage she hoped to see more of them, hoped that they too would become part of her life.

But nothing could replace Rosa and she

looked at her sister now with a twinge of anxiety at the thought of leaving her, knew how much she would miss her.

Reading her expression, Rosa gave her a gentle smile. 'I'll miss you, but maybe one day Father *will* let me visit you and Marco.'

Sofia frowned. That had been one point King Fiero had been immovable on.

'Your sister is free to call you but she will not be visiting. Rosa's position is now of even more importance and I will not allow her to leave Palosia at this time.'

Somehow the words had sounded ominous, made her wonder what her father had planned for her sister. A marriage, of course, but a marriage to whom?

On impulse, she reached out and took Rosa's hand in hers. 'Rosa. I won't presume to tell you what to do. But I wish, I hope, that you find the same happiness I have.'

Her sister vouchsafed no answer, her brown eyes unreadable. Then she smiled, a smile so sweet it twisted Sofia's heart.

'Right now, it is your happiness I am thinking about; this is your day, Sofia, and all I want today is to see my sister marry the man she loves and start her happy ever after. So, let's go, before Marco starts to worry. And here is your bouquet.'

Sofia took the flowers her sister had chosen and arranged, a glorious concoction made up of the pink and creamy roses that her sister grew and cultivated with such care, daisies and gypsophila, interspersed with sweet peas, lavender and jasmine, the resultant scent somehow redolent of sunshine and happiness. Sofia gave her sister a massive hug.

'Thank you. They are beautiful. Truly perfect.' She stood still as Rosa made a few last-minute adjustments and then they left, exited the palace into the horse-drawn carriage that took them to the palace chapel. Happiness suffused Sofia as she arrived at the entrance to the ancient stone church, waited for her father to step out of his own carriage to join her.

And as the music started all other thoughts and considerations were gone. She walked forward, her eyes firmly fixed on Marco, and when she saw his arresting look, saw his grey eyes light up as she took each step closer, her heart skipped exultantly, filled with happiness and joy and love as she reached the man she loved so very, very much. Her prince, her happy ever after.

* * * * *

Get up to 4 Free Books!

We'll send you 2 free books from each series you try
PLUS a free Mystery Gift.

FREE Value Over **$25**

Both the **Harlequin® Historical** and **Harlequin® Romance** series feature compelling novels filled with emotion and simmering romance.

YES! Please send me 2 FREE novels from the Harlequin Historical or Harlequin Romance series and my FREE Mystery Gift (gift is worth about $10 retail). After receiving them, if I don't wish to receive any more books, I can return the shipping statement marked "cancel." If I don't cancel, I will receive 5 brand-new Harlequin Historical books every month and be billed just $6.39 each in the U.S. or $7.19 each in Canada, or 4 brand-new Harlequin Romance Larger-Print books every month and be billed just $7.19 each in the U.S. or $7.99 each in Canada, a savings of 20% off the cover price. It's quite a bargain! Shipping and handling is just 50¢ per book in the U.S. and $1.25 per book in Canada.* I understand that accepting the 2 free books and gift places me under no obligation to buy anything. I can always return a shipment and cancel at any time by calling the number below. The free books and gift are mine to keep no matter what I decide.

Choose one: ☐ **Harlequin Historical** (246/349 BPA G36Y) ☐ **Harlequin Romance Larger-Print** (119/319 BPA G36Y) ☐ **Or Try Both!** (246/349 & 119/319 BPA G36Z)

Name (please print)

Address   Apt. #

City   State/Province   Zip/Postal Code

Email: Please check this box ☐ if you would like to receive newsletters and promotional emails from Harlequin Enterprises ULC and its affiliates. You can unsubscribe anytime.

Mail to the **Harlequin Reader Service:**
IN U.S.A.: P.O. Box 1341, Buffalo, NY 14240-8531
IN CANADA: P.O. Box 603, Fort Erie, Ontario L2A 5X3

Want to explore our other series or interested in ebooks? Visit www.ReaderService.com or call 1-800-873-8635.

---

*Terms and prices subject to change without notice. Prices do not include sales taxes, which will be charged (if applicable) based on your state or country of residence. Canadian residents will be charged applicable taxes. Offer not valid in Quebec. This offer is limited to one order per household. Books received may not be as shown. Not valid for current subscribers to the Harlequin Historical or Harlequin Romance series. All orders subject to approval. Credit or debit balances in a customer's account(s) may be offset by any other outstanding balance owed by or to the customer. Please allow 4 to 6 weeks for delivery. Offer available while quantities last.

Your Privacy—Your information is being collected by Harlequin Enterprises ULC, operating as Harlequin Reader Service. For a complete summary of the information we collect, how we use this information and to whom it is disclosed, please visit our privacy notice located at https://corporate.harlequin.com/privacy-notice. Notice to California Residents – Under California law, you have specific rights to control and access your data. For more information on these rights and how to exercise them, visit https://corporate.harlequin.com/california-privacy. For additional information for residents of other U.S. states that provide their residents with certain rights with respect to personal data, visit https://corporate.harlequin.com/other-state-residents-privacy-rights/.

HHHRLP25